# THE PRETTY ONES

# THE PRETTY ONES

## JAMIE LEE FRY

**BIG**MOUNTAIN
— PUBLISHING —

# THE PRETTY ONES
## JAMIE LEE FRY

Barnes & Noble edition ISBN: 978-1-7371202-2-3
Print edition ISBN: 978-1-7371202-0-9
E-book edition ISBN: 978-1-7371202-1-6

First edition: AUGUST 2021
10 9 8 7 6 5 4 3 2 1

## WWW.AUTHORJAMIELEEFRY.COM

FOR JEREMY, WITH LOVE

# PART ONE

# CHAPTER 01

## *Charlie*
## *August 2012*

Something is wrong. Something is definitely wrong.

I glance over to an empty bottle of vodka on the seat next to me. Is that mine? My memory is a blur.

My head is foggy and the throbbing in my temples is unbearable. I can't think. I swear I hear my pulse beating within me like my ears are going to explode.

The hot sun bounces off the car and hits me in the face. I wither back like a vampire.

Something is wrong.

I push the palms of my hands hard against my eyes and rub them in a circular motion, searching for clarity. I remove my hands, and the street ahead of me comes into focus. Tall ponderosa pine trees line both sides of the street. The bluebird sky is full above, and my heart drops to the pit of my tummy. I know exactly where I am.

I should not be here. This is bad.

I don't remember coming here.

My heart feels like it is going to leap out of my chest. The dry air makes it hard to swallow, but I manage to push down the bile that's rising in my throat. It burns.

I can't be here. I have to go. I can't go down this road again. That was four years ago.

I reach forward to start my car. I have to leave before anyone catches me parked here. People will talk. People always talk. My hand shakes as I turn the key that's thankfully in the ignition.

Oh, no. No, no, no. Is that Zoey McKinley jogging across the street?

She can't see me here. I slide down in my seat.

It's too late. Zoey waves her hand excitedly toward me.

"Charlie, is that you?" Zoey yells.

I glance up into my rearview mirror. A ghostly, unrecognizable face stares back at me. I pat down the mess that is my straggly dishwater-blonde hair and tuck the sides behind my ears. My blue eyes are glazed over and growing redder by the second. I wipe the smeared mascara from under my eyes and pinch my cheeks to give them some color.

I watch Zoey as she rounds my car, careful that she doesn't notice I'm moving an empty vodka bottle under my passenger seat.

"Charlie," Zoey shouts. "It is you!"

Zoey is happy to see me. I wish I could say the same.

She is standing next to my car now, motioning for me to roll down my window. She hasn't changed a bit.

The brisk morning air invades my vehicle as I obey her gesture. I welcome the fresh air, but I'm sorry for whatever scents are flowing out the window toward my old friend.

"Hey, Zoey. It's been a while. Good to see you," I say. My voice doesn't sound genuine and it's slightly groggy. Normally, I would be happy to reconnect, but Zoey has caught me at a bad time.

Zoey is just as peppy as I remember. She still has a little bounce in her step. I'm glad to see the past four years were good to her, but right now is not the time.

"I haven't seen you since . . ." She stops mid-sentence; most people do because they forget how to handle it. After all, it's been over four years.

"I wasn't sure it was actually you. But your green VW Beetle is a dead giveaway. I have missed this car and I've missed you. How have you been, Charlie?" Zoey is genuine with her words and always has been.

"I've been good," I say. I'm lying. Clearly, I look like hell. I'm not fine.

"You never called me back after everything happened. I eventually had to stop trying. I wanted to be there for you, Charlie. You didn't let me in. I think about you often," Zoey said empathetically.

I frown. I don't want to talk about that. I change the subject. "Do you live around here now?" I ask Zoey.

"Yah, I've got an apartment one street over, near the park," Zoey responds as she points in the direction of her new home. "So, whatcha doin' over here?" She rocks back and forth on her heels, keeping her high energy going. Her auburn ponytail sways with her.

A bird chirps in a tree nearby. *Chirp. Chirp.* It doesn't stop. I can't think. How should I answer this?

*Chirp. Chirp.*

As if in slow motion, I watch sweet Zoey put the pieces together. She looks behind her to the sage-green house that sits further back from the street and then swiftly back at me.

I fidget in my seat and wait for it.

"Charlie, you shouldn't be here. Ya know Liam doesn't live here anymore, but you know what people will say if they see your car parked out front. You really should go. Let's get coffee sometime and catch up. Mike is back in town, too. I know he would love to see you. But sweetie, you need to go." Zoey gives me air hugs and turns back to the sidewalk and jogs away.

Zoey is right. I have to go.

# CHAPTER 02

### *Charlie*
### *August 2012*

I park my car outside my parents' house, barely remembering the drive home. Maybe I should have called a cab. I don't feel drunk, but I'm definitely hungover.

I don't recall drinking last night, but the empty bottle and the throbbing headache suggest otherwise.

What am I going to do with myself? I sigh and pull my phone from my purse to text Quinn.

> *Quinn. I miss you—I wish you would forgive me. What did I do to you? I need a friend right now. I need you.*

I immediately delete it.

I sneak past through the yard and in through our backdoor. This entrance to our home has always had a creak to it, even when moved slowly. I cringe as I carefully swing the door open, hoping to avoid detection and silence the creak as much as possible.

Fail. The creak has gotten worse with age. A dead giveaway to my presence.

I'm a twenty-two-year-old woman sneaking into her parents' house. Let's chalk the entire morning up to a new all-time low. I leave my sneakers on the rug and tiptoe into the kitchen and open the door that leads to the garage. Both cars gone. Mom and Dad must have left for work already. In that moment I realize I honestly have no idea what time it is and actually don't care. I'm just relieved I don't have to explain myself and get to avoid my mom's classic look of disappointment. I know the look all too well.

I would have to explain to them that their investment in me and their hard-earned money spent on my college education is going to have to wait another day. I've let the entire summer slip by without any luck of a job worth noting. Everything has been kind of a blur since I've been back. I didn't have the forethought to line anything up before I left college, so now I'm living back in Bend, Oregon, with my parents. I can't lie to myself; it has been nice living rent free and having zero responsibility, but that also comes with increased pressure. The throbbing intensifies, and I know it's time for some sleep. I will sort things out later.

Add job hunt to tomorrows to-do list.

I gather a couple Advil and a glass of water and head straight for my bedroom.

I crawl into my familiar bed. The first time I've felt safe all morning. I wrap myself tight in my blanket and stare around my room. My entire bedroom is exactly as I left it four years ago. The pale-blue walls are littered with photos of me and my best friends Zoey and Mike. Oh, sweet Zoey. I feel bad about this morning. I will have to call her and explain. On second thought, I'm not sure what I will explain because I don't understand how I got there or why I was even there in the first place. I shut Zoey out all those years ago. I couldn't face anyone after what happened to Aunt Jenny. Zoey did nothing wrong. I pushed her away. Zoey tried back then and was nothing but thoughtful and kind to me and my family. She was worried about me all those years ago; and it's clear she still has my back today. Sweet, kind Zoey.

Everything about my room reminds me I was a different person before everything went to shit. I close my eyes and hope for sleep, but images appear like a movie reel, flashing on the back of my heavy eyelids. Flashes of Jenny whimsically dancing around my room as her chestnut-brown hair bounces effortlessly. Her smile, her laugh; I see and hear it, like she's still here with me.

I want to keep these visions as long as I can. I squeeze my eyes tight, trying to impress them against the back of my eyes. It never works but I always try. My eyelids involuntarily flutter. I push harder to stop them from changing scenes, but I know what's coming next.

Rapid waves of crimson rush against my eyes. I try to open them, but they're heavily weighted.

Jenny screams.

# CHAPTER 03

### Charlie
### August 2012

Slivers of sunlight warm my face as I lie securely wrapped in my blanket and soak up the warmth and fieriness the sun graces upon me. I know these little glimmers of sunshine will be the best part of my day. I stretch my arms out, embracing the feeling of tension releasing in my limbs. That nap was a good idea. I really needed that. I've been so off lately. Not quite myself.

A realization clocks into my sleep-addled brain. I turn my head to check out the clock on my nightstand; bright red numbers display 09:02. I slept through the entire day and night? I furrow my brows in confusion and rub the grit from my eyes. Gosh, I must have been tired after yesterday's unplanned outing. Maybe that's it; I just needed a couple more hours sleep and now I feel right as rain. I just needed a recharge. Everything will be OK. I just need to keep myself busy today to avoid a repeat of yesterday. Whatever that was. It can't happen again. It's probably best if I just stay home today. I pull the covers over my head and give myself more time in bed. Thinking. Processing.

When I venture outside the house, I feel the darkness that my hometown has created for me. My own personal hell. I wish my parents had moved away when I left for college. I know we live in one of the most beautiful cities in the country, but how can any of us enjoy it anymore? Our sunny, beautiful, desert-mountain town is now tainted for me. Everything stirs up a memory and it's too hard to bear. Every restaurant, hiking trail, running trail, corner of our house, even the beautiful cascade mountain range makes me sad or angry depending on the day. Things that used to bring me joy now only stir up memories and it hurts. I can't go anywhere without thinking of Jenny.

I have to keep busy, keep my mind off things. I need to apply for jobs far away from here. Maybe I should do that today.

The thought overwhelms me as much as staying here, but who am I kidding? I probably won't end up doing that today.

I'm kind of surprised my parents didn't bother to wake me. Probably just used to their time alone now. Their routines have changed. I'm guessing that's all it is. I feel like I haven't seen them in days. Dad stays busy at the office and Mom has her floral shop downtown to take care of. Mom and Dad found new ways to connect after I left. They took cooking classes, dance lessons, and even learned to ski. I'm happy for them but don't understand how they can endure the darkness and come out seemly normal now. They don't talk about her much. I suppose it's easier that way.

I wait until the sun is fully introduced to my room before I get out of bed. I have the whole day ahead of me. Gotta keep busy, I keep reminding myself.

I reach for my phone. No new messages. I want to text Quinn.

Instead, I wander around my room and take inventory as I walk about, mentally jotting down the things I should change if

I'm going to stay. I know I need to leave sooner than later, but the inevitability of me staying is looking more likely each day since I keep putting off the job hunt. I may as well have a fresh start with a clean slate. Might as well start with my room.

Posters of my favorite bands are scattered throughout the room, mixed in with my high-school photos.

All of that needs to come down.

Row after row of books line the bookshelves my dad made for me. My books make me happy and bring me joy, so those will stay, but the old CD player sitting atop one of the shelves has to go. Do people even have CDs anymore? I pick up a Panic! At the Disco album and put it into the dusty old CD player. I used to love this album. A little bit of happy nostalgia is welcomed right now. Upbeat music fills the room, slightly lifting my mood. The knots are still in my belly from yesterday, but I ignore them and continue on.

Gotta keep busy.

Sweet childhood stuffed animals sit one on top of one another in my green papasan chair, making it nearly unusable. I pull a tattered monkey out and toss it on the floor and manage to wedge my butt into the chair. All these have to go. Nestled in a mess of stuffed memories, I take notice of my closet. One side is lined with high-school T-shirts, sweatshirts, and Converse shoes. The other side is fancy tops, sweaters, and high heels. The drastic difference of my two lives. The only evidence of my life at the University of Iowa. I had sold nearly all of my other belongings before moving back to Oregon. It was too much of a hassle to move the things that curated my life there. I only took home with me what would fit in a couple suitcases.

Quinn would cringe if she saw the older half of my closet; little does she know I've only been wearing my sneakers and T-shirts since I've been back. I'm OK with cozy over cute these days.

My oak desk is lined with framed family photos.

That's strange. I get up and head toward my desk.

One of the frames is turned face-down. I must have bumped it coming in yesterday. I pick the frame up and see it's one of me and Jenny.

I remember the day it was taken. It was her college graduation. Aunt Jenny in her black cap and gown with her orange sash, smiling from ear to ear. I'm tucked in her tight embrace. I remember thinking I was going to follow in her footsteps and attend Oregon State. I almost did too, but I couldn't after what happened.

The knots in my tummy churn again, and I wince in pain. I hit stop on the CD player and take the frame back to the chair with me. I study the picture some more. Gosh, Jenny was so pretty. She was absolutely perfect. I wish I could be more like her. I miss her deeply.

We were so close. Jenny was more like a sister to me than an aunt, and being an only child, I ate up all her attention. I was lonely when she wasn't around. She really was my best friend. I say Mike and Zoey were my best friends, but they were my high-school besties and we stuck together because we were slight outcasts and it was convenient for us to all be friends at school. But Jenny, she was my confidant. I looked up to her. She was sixteen when I was born but despite the age difference, she totally got me.

She left such a void in my life. Life isn't fair sometimes.

I feel the darkness coming back, and I have to shut it down before it takes control. It was easier to forget in Iowa, with my shield of distance. I wish I had planned better and stayed there.

I have to shut down this tunnel I'm heading toward. I can't do this today. Sorry, Jenny.

I hug the frame and give it a sweet kiss. I miss you, Jenny. I put her picture back in its proper place and grab my phone. I want to text Quinn.

> *Quinn, hey girl. Thinking of you. I want to talk about what happened that night. I miss you.*

I delete it.

# CHAPTER 04

## Charlie
## August 2012

A familiar feeling of the sun burning along my face tickles me awake. My mouth parched from the dry heat of the high-desert air, a huge change from the Midwestern humid summers. I desperately reach for the cup of water on my nightstand and chug the entire glass. The lukewarm contents soothe my dry throat.

I felt satisfied with the work I did on my bedroom yesterday, and I need to keep busy today, but I'm not sure what to do with my time. I've got nothing but time these days.

OK, Charlie. Today you have to do something productive. This is the best pep talk I can muster up. I force myself out of my queen-sized bed and slip my feet into my fuzzy blue slippers and head for the kitchen.

Looks like the parentals are at work.

My stomach grumbles, and I try to recall the last thing I ate. Nothing comes to mind. I really need to start taking better care of myself. How did I survive the last four years? I'm clearly winning at adulting.

I grab the bread from the pantry, undo the twist tie, and plop two slices of bread in the toaster. As I wait for my breakfast, I space out and lose a little bit of time. The ejection of the toast startles me and pulls me back to reality. The smell of nearly burnt toast fills the air. I grab the butter but opt to forgo the peanut butter because it feels like too much work.

I'm picking at my breakfast when my phone starts ringing upstairs.

I rush through the kitchen and down the hallway. It's still ringing. I have a chance to answer it. I run up the steps and as my feet hit the landing, the ringing stops. Shoot.

*One missed call.*

*Quinn.*

I wait impatiently for a voicemail.

Nothing.

I've been waiting for this call all summer and I miss it by just seconds. You got to be kidding me. Just my luck.

I pace the room. Do I call her back? It has been an entire summer without her. I can't explain it, but really need her right now. I've been a mess without her.

I decide to wait fifteen minutes before I call her back. I don't want her to think I've been sitting by my phone the past three months, waiting for her to finally get in touch.

The phone rings multiple times before I get her voicemail. Dammit.

I stumble for my words. I should have prepared them before calling.

"Um, hi, Quinn. Um, I saw you called. I missed it. Obviously." I laugh nervously. "I haven't heard from you all summer. I was happy to see you called. You can, um, call me back. I would love to talk to you. OK, bye now." I end the call.

Ugh. I'm so mad I missed her call. I stare at my phone, willing it to ring again.

Nothing happens.

# CHAPTER 05

## Charlie
## August 2012

I wake up in a fog. Once again, my memory a blur. The flavor of death coats my mouth. I smack my lips to create some movement and saliva, but my efforts are futile.

Comprehension arrives a moment later. Shit! I did it again. The familiar street, the same tall trees, the sage-green house.

I'm parked outside Liam's old house again. Shit.

Before I can even give way to a single coherent thought, I turn my car on and yank the steering wheel toward the street. A half-empty bottle of vodka rolls off the seat and hits the floor. Crap, crap, crap. What is going on with me? I drive my car down a couple of blocks and pull over on a side street. I move the bottle into the trunk and then get back into my car.

I bang my hands furiously against the dashboard and scream in horror. "Come on, Charlie, come on, get a grip. Get a damn hold of yourself, girl!" I pinch the skin between my pointer finger and thumb to see if I feel anything. I need to know if I'm dreaming or if I'm really here in this moment. A sharp tingle runs down the middle of my hand. OK, I feel something, so what does that prove? Am I losing my mind? How did I get here again and when did I decide it was a good idea to drink? I can't recall a single memory from last night. I glance down and I appear to be wearing Jenny's OSU sweatshirt. I don't remember putting this on. Where did this sweatshirt come from?

An obnoxious rattle jolts my attention to my armrest. Something inside is rapidly knocking back and forth. I need this noise to stop now. I can barely think straight as it is. I don't need any distractions. I open the console and I see my phone vibrating inside. My attempt to silence the call fails as I accidentally hit answer instead of silence.

I impulsively holler, "What?" into the phone. My response startles and disappoints me immediately. I sink deeper into my seat. Fear of not knowing who I rudely spoke to unnerves me.

"Excuse me. Um, Charlie? Is that you?" A soft, recognizable voice expresses confusion and concern.

Oh my goodness. It's Quinn. Poor timing. This is not how I imagined reconnecting with her.

Say something, Charlie. Speak, dammit. I take a deep breath to gather a little bit of composure.

"Oh, hey, Quinn. Yes, it's me. Sorry, I didn't realize it was you calling," I say, careful with my words. I don't want to say the wrong thing and mess this conversation up. I need Quinn now more than ever, but she needs to believe I'm OK before I unload everything on her.

"Did I catch you at a bad time? Are you doing, OK? You sound off," Quinn says with worry in her voice.

It is nice to hear she is concerned but I choke back the words I really want to say. I take a deep breath in an attempt to gain a little bit of composure.

"No, no, it's all good. I'm glad you called back. How are you?" I reply with a generic response, but what I really want to say is I feel like I'm stuck on a loop like I'm in *Groundhog Day*. Oh, and I may or may not be drunk right now and I'm losing my mind. But I don't say any of that.

"I'm doing well," she responds, unphased by my monotone response. "I took a summer internship in Seattle, but I'm back in Portland now. I thought we could meet and talk. Can you head over here tomorrow?" Quinn asks.

"Ah, sure, that sounds nice. Should I meet you at your parents' house?" I hear the lack of energy in my voice.

Put on a better show, Charlie. Quinn can usually see through my bullshit. She's bold and brass when she needs to be.

"Oh, no, don't go there. My parents are busy doing some remodeling at our house and it's a mess. Let's meet downtown. I'm sure you will want to hit up Powell's bookstore, so why don't we just meet there. Let's say noon?" Quinn says.

"That sounds good," I respond, with a little more pep in my words.

"Hey, Charlie? Are you sure you're doing, OK?" Quinn asks.

"Yah, I'm doing fine. I will fill you in tomorrow," I say. I want to tell Quinn nothing has been the same since I saw her last, but instead, I opt for a simple, "See ya tomorrow."

"OK, Charlie. See ya tomorrow." Quinn says and ends the call.

And just like that, the conversation I have been waiting for all summer is over. No word about what happened that fateful night. Zero mention of the evening I don't remember.

# CHAPTER 06

### Charlie
### August 2012

My anxiety was high yesterday after Quinn called. I was excited but anxious about seeing her again. It was all I could think about. It didn't give my mind the space it needed to sort through my other issues. I can save that for my return from Portland. One problem at a time is all I can handle today. It also looks like the job hunt will have to be postponed as well.

It was nearly eight thirty when I realized Mom and Dad used up the last of the coffee and left me none. How dare they? Don't they understand my codependency with coffee? They didn't even bother to leave me a note. I will need to make a stop for some on my way out of town. I now have less time to dillydally around, so I better get out the door or I will be late. Nothing irritates Quinn more than tardiness. It's OK for her to be tardy, but no one else.

\*\*\*

I must have been on autopilot as I find myself in the Coffee Loon parking lot across from my former high school. Old habits die hard, don't they? The school looks smaller than I remember. Maybe the trees grew taller? The ancient-looking juniper trees line the entire perimeter of the property creating an uninviting atmosphere.

I'm grateful my time there is over.

During my junior and senior years, I escaped nearly every lunch break and walked over to the Coffee Loon for a midday snack and pick-me-up. I looked forward to my little break each day, but now I can't bring myself to get out of the car. This once happy escape is now coated with dark memories. Memories of lunchtime coffee dates with Liam.

That was before he . . .

No, Charlie, don't go there. Not today.

I immediately shut down the dark thoughts that are about to invade my memory.

Thankfully, our growing and booming town has more than enough room for a second coffee shop on the street. I spot a new sign at the end of the block.

*Cuppa Mud Coffee House.*

Score. Someone is looking out for me today.

I walk down to the end of the street toward the new café.

"New beginnings," I say under my breath and step inside.

Empty burlap coffee sacks hang on the walls. Simple but effective decor. Only a couple of small tables for two line the windows, suggesting they would rather have you take your coffee to-go. Only one of the tables is occupied. A girl with an open laptop facing the rear of the store. I'm greeted with the pleasant scent of homemade blueberry scones and freshly brewed coffee. I didn't plan to order a pastry, but now I'm enticed to do so. I step up to the counter and an older woman with her hair slicked tightly back in a bun welcomes me. Her name tag reads Darla. Darla smiles, her teeth coffee stained.

"Hi, dear, what can I get for ya this morning?" she asks.

"I would love one of your blueberry scones and a large Americano," I say with certainty.

"Room for cream in your Americano?" Darla asks.

No, black is good. Fill 'er up," I say.

"I like your style. That's how I drink mine, too. No frills," Darla says, looking pleased with her comment.

I chuckle. "I worked at a coffee house in college, and I couldn't get through my shift and the following classes without at least one of these bad boys per day." I think Darla's enjoying our banter.

She smiles and continues with the small talk. "Which coffee house did ya work at?"

"Oh, it wasn't around here. It was called the Java Hut in Iowa." I respond.

"Never been there myself, but I had an uncle who lived in Iowa for a short stint. He always complained about the weather. I never went for a visit. Why would I? He made the place sound miserable. He eventually moved to South Carolina. Now that's a place to visit," Darla says.

"I get it. Cold winters, hot summers. I understand why he left." I reach for some napkins and tuck some into my pocket for the drive.

"That'll be eight dollars fifty, hun."

I hand her a ten. "Keep the change," I say.

"Thanks, dear. Coffee's just about up, scone will be a sec. Got some fresh ones 'bout to come out of the oven. Best scones in Bend, I tell ya."

The barista hands Darla my coffee and she hands it over to me.

"Here's your coffee, doll. Big plans today?"

Darla's chattiness doesn't seem to create a sense of urgency, but I glance behind me anyway to make sure I'm not holding up the line. A man in khakis and a button-up shirt is standing off to the side assessing the menu like he's never been to a coffee house before. His pointer finger resting on his chin as if he's in deep thought. I imagine he's going to order a frilly drink. Mocha perhaps. I used to love guessing people's drink orders before they placed them. I was pretty good at it, too.

"Heading to Portland to see a friend," I respond back.

A second worker comes out from the back and hands Darla my scone in a little white bag.

"Here ya go, dear. Have a good drive. Weather's supposed to be nice today," Darla says.

"Thanks. See ya next time." This is the most I've interacted with someone in days. I appreciate Darla's kindness. I will definitely be back.

The man behind me doesn't even give me a second to step out of the way. He's already at the register, standing next to me, ready to place his order.

I take my time exiting the building, walking slowly so I can hear his order.

Darla says, "What cha having, sweetie?"

"Mocha frap with extra chocolate sprinkles, please," the man says.

Yep. That's what I thought. I still got it. I giggle as I walk out of the building.

Breakfast. Check. Coffee. Check. Three hours alone in a car with my thoughts. This won't be good.

# CHAPTER 07

### Charlie
### October 2008

The air is cool and damp. Fallen leaves cake the sidewalk. None of the businesses have swept yet—it's too early. The wind is brisk as it whooshes past me. I retreat further into the doorway. A couple of freshly fallen leaves dance by. I check my phone again for the time. 4:01 a.m. Gavin is late. In the two months I've worked here, I've never had to wait outside; Gavin's usually here by now with the lights on and ready to bark orders.

The Java Hut is situated on a busy street in the pedestrian mall. Although, a mall it hardly is. I've been told this area used to be a busy shopping center in the eighties, but now it's a blend of University of Iowa buildings, restaurants, obscure shops, and bars. Our block is oddly curated with a bookstore, a candy shop, comic-book store, an upscale restaurant, and finally ends with a late-night burrito joint, that stays open until three in the morning. Sometimes when I come into work, I see the tired souls of the late-night restaurant workers ending their shift and walking to their cars. I feel so bad for them. They have to serve drunk college kids all night, and I'm sure they get little respect from any of them. I once saw a drunk guy puke in their garbage can and then on the floor. This drunken act was not uncommon. I was delighted I was lucky to work at a coffee shop, even if I started at 4 a.m. I was notably exhausted all the time, and school had been kicking my butt already. High school was a cakewalk compared to college life.

The entire street behind the Java Hut is more consistent, as it is home to more bars, taverns, pubs, and dance clubs than any one college should have. I'm not sure how any college student survives four years here. I haven't had much time to party yet. Being a freshman who lives off campus doesn't help.

I've made no real friends yet. I pretty much just know my co-workers, and I wouldn't call us friends. They have invited me to a couple of parties; I have only gone to one but left early. They are pleasant at work, but outside work, I'm invisible to them.

I check the time again. Only a few minutes have passed. I want to text Gavin, but I never got around to saving his phone number in my phone. The store phone list they gave me at orientation is still sitting in my work locker. A lot of good it's doing me there right now. Hindsight is twenty-twenty.

The morning is quiet. I'm always in too big of a rush to take notice how calm downtown can be this early in the morning. It's very peaceful, but the darkness at this hour creates an eerie feeling at the same time. Downtown comes to life around 8 a.m. with college students, professors, and locals rushing about preparing for their day, creating an entirely different feel. Everything is rushed and busy and loud once the day gets rolling.

"Come on, Gavin. Where are you?" I mumble out loud to myself and I see my breath float by. My teeth begin to chatter, and the wind picks up. I'm feeling anxious now. I check my phone for the third time. 4:10. I want to leave but I know the second I do, Gavin will show up and I will be the one in trouble for missing my shift. I'm now alert to all the little noises of the street. The ticking of a crosswalk alerts a twelve-second countdown. Trees are rustling in the wind. I'm getting more and more irritated with Gavin's tardiness and I'm about to leave when I hear a rattle from a few store fronts down. I carefully peek around the corner to see what's creating the obnoxious noise that's out of place for this time of morning. A bum emerges from an empty doorway and is now coming down my side of the street. He's pushing a cart with one hand while the other hand tightly grips a brown bag. He stops and takes a sip from the contents of the bag. I assume it's alcohol. As he gets closer, loose cans rattle louder against the metal cart. I tuck myself further into the doorway. I'm pressed hard against the cold glass door. The bum stops again, now directly in front of me. He doesn't take any notice but pulls another swig. His tattered brown jacket and ill-fitting pants flap in the wind, wafting a smell of urine, cigarettes, and stale booze. A chill runs down my entire spine. I want to vomit, but I hold my composure. He continues on without noticing me. He whistles his way down the street and the clanking of his cans get louder as the sidewalk gets rougher and uneven until it fades back out as he lurks into another doorway.

An anxious sensation sweeps through my body. I should feel relieved now that he is out of sight, but I feel panicky. My eyes begin to flutter and I'm shivering from the cold. I need this job, but I can feel my heart racing with terror and I'm a little freaked out right now. Gavin should understand. He's the one who's late. I take off running down the street toward the bus stop. I turn my head over my shoulder to make sure no one is behind me and my body slams hard up against something or someone.

I'm afraid to look up, but then I hear a familiar voice.

"Whoa, Charlie, where ya going?" Gavin says, concerned.

"Oh my, Gavin, you scared the hell out of me. I didn't know if you were still coming. It's way after four. Where have you been?" I say.

"Ya, sorry. Alarm didn't go off," Gavin admits. "Sorry, I should've called you."

You think? Geez. "I was getting a little freaked out," I tell him. "A bum gave me a little scare, and I didn't know if you were coming."

"Oh, the bums are harmless. You probably ran into Lester. He's an old vet that hangs around our street. Surprised you haven't seen him yet. He sleeps in the doorways until morning and then moves into the park during the day. He has his vices, but he's completely harmless," Gavin says.

Before I know it, we've walked back to the store. Gavin unlocks the door and unarms the alarm.

I cannot help but feel anxious still. I know everything is fine now, but I'm overwhelmed, and I want to go home. I know I should stay. I need the extra money. My parents pay for my off-campus apartment and most of my expenses, but I want to help contribute as much as I can. I don't want them to worry about me. It was hard enough convincing them I would be OK on my own after what happened with Jenny. I want to prove to them I can be independent. If my parents knew I was working this much, they probably would ask me to quit and tell me they would send a bigger allowance, but I can't ask that of them. I really don't mind it here that much and it helps keep my mind busy.

Gavin is buzzing around the shop, preparing to open any minute now. Since he was late, we are cutting it close. I can see Gavin's mood changing. He was rushed and sympathetic earlier, but now he's in bossy work mode and Gavin is not a morning person. I've never known Gavin to be late, but now I find myself wondering how often this happens. Gavin is in his late twenties. He started working at the Java Hut when he was in college. He never ended up graduating and found himself moving up the "java ladder" until he was the boss. I think he begrudged all the college kids that came through and moved on with their degrees at the end of each school year. Gavin probably was a more cheerful person when he was younger, but grew grumpier and more resentful as he aged. While he is doing his opening routine, I sneak over to the espresso machine and pretend I'm preparing it for the morning, but really, I'm pouring myself a shot. I gulp it down before Gavin notices. Gavin doesn't drink coffee. How can you run a coffee shop and not drink coffee? I, on the other hand, have always used coffee like a lifeline. I probably drink too much. I couldn't survive a day without it.

The warm shot of espresso gives me the jolt I need, but I feel even more anxious now.

"Charlie!" Gavin yells from the backroom.

His voice startles me. I jump.

"Those lazy college student friends of yours left you a mess again. Can you take out the trash before we open? We can't have this garbage stacking up back here. What if OSHA comes today?"

That was always his phrase: "What if OSHA comes today?"

Yes, it is true, Occupational Safety and Health Administration could come today, but would they really?

Nothing makes Gavin grumpier than the closing team leaving trash for the openers. I should be the grumpy one. I'm the one cleaning up after them.

"It's time to open. Can I just wait until eight when Anna comes in?" I ask. I really do not want to go back outside. I was out there all dang morning waiting for his grumpy ass.

"No, it has to get done before opening," Gavin says and he motions me away. He has rounded the corner before I can say another word.

"Jerk." I will just take my sweet time then, secretly willing a quicker sunrise, as I have never felt comfortable taking out the trash in the dark. I walk slowly, slugging my feet along the floor. I prop the backdoor open into the alley. I reach down to gather the trash piled up by the door and haul my first load outside. The entire alleyway is quite interesting. Murals line the entire backside of our buildings, attempting to create some magic in an ugly area. A giant red heart being gripped by a hand with three drops of blood dripping down is depicted behind the trash compactor. Odd choice but each artist was given free rein to do whatever they wanted.

I toss one bag of trash over at a time. I go back for the last two I left in the doorway. One bag slips from my hand and it splits right down the side, with all the gooey contents spilling out over the pavement. I bend down to attempt to do my best to retrieve the trash and open the second bag to combine the two.

Foul, stale booze invades the air. I examine the trash and the smell is not coming from the split bag.

I hurry to finish my task. I have had enough of the outside this morning.

The smell is closing in. Maybe it's harmless Lester circling back around before heading into the park.

"Lester, is that you?" I say cautiously.

No response. Must be my imagination.

I continue to gather the stinky trash contents and I hear a rustle from behind me. Not my imagination. Fuck.

My body stiffens and fear takes over my entire being. I can't move.

"Gavin? Lester? Who's there?" I ask, but not brave enough to actually turn my head and look.

Please be a raccoon. Please be a raccoon.

Another foul whiff creeps past me. The Odor of beer and cigarettes stings my nostrils. A figure creeps from behind the dumpster and is moving toward me. It's not Lester or Gavin.

Fear still paralyzing me, all I can do is let out a shriek. My mind is screaming to run, but my feet won't budge.

The figure doesn't speak but continues in my direction. It reaches out toward me. I close my eyes. It's all I can think to do.

"Please go away," I repeat to myself. "Please go away." The figure is leaning over my body when I open my eyes. I shut them tight again. "Please go away." Images of Jenny flash through my memories.

I can't seem to catch my breath. I suck in air but all I can do is push the breath out faster in a panic. My chest is thumping.

My feet unlock below, releasing me, and I fall back onto the pavement. I scoot my entire body back against the bleeding-heart wall. My eyes remaining closed. "Go away." Involuntarily, my body rocks against the mural. "Go away," I cry out.

I bravely open one eye and there is no one there. I close my eyes and shut them both tight as I coach myself through my panicky breathing. Breathe, Charlie, breathe. In, out.

I deeply inhale and once again booze, urine, and cigarettes sting my nostrils. Another chill runs the length of my back and the hair on my arms stands erect.

A hand taps my shoulder. I shuddered back further toward the wall. "no, no, no." I scream.

"Ma'am. You OK?" A raspy old voice shouts at me.

I open my eyes. It's Lester.

How did he get here? Was he here the whole time? I know

it wasn't Lester that I just saw. I would've recognized these tattered clothes.

"Hey, girl, what got you spooked? Ain't no one here," Lester asks, interrupting my thoughts.

I say nothing, but stare blankly at him. I'm confused and frightened, but yet I know it wasn't this man.

Lester smiles a toothless grin at me and says, "Go on, git inside girl. Ain't nothing here." He points toward the open backdoor then reaches down to sift through my open trash bag.

I get up and run inside and pull the heavy door securely shut behind me. I'm panting like a dog trying to control my breath.

I let the entire weight of my body rest against the door, and I continue to catch my breath. Tears stream down my face.

I hear Gavin around the corner. I pat my eyes to dry them quickly.

"Geez, Charlie, what took ya so long. I was about to come looking for ya," Gavin says as he catches me wiping my face. "What's wrong with you?" he asks with very little concern.

"I just got dizzy. I need to go home," I lie to him. I don't know how to really answer his question. I'm not sure what is wrong with me. I've been spooked since he was late this morning and I saw something I can't explain in the darkness. I already ran into him like a crazy person this morning.

Gavin walks over to the schedule and pulls it off the corkboard. He examines it and says, "Can you wait until Anna gets here at eight? I can't cover the morning all by myself." He frowns at me.

"I guess so," I say sadly.

"Go wash your hands and get out to the floor. I've only had a couple customers so far, but it's about to get busy. It's almost five o'clock," Gavin says.

The bell on the door dings and chatter between two women

fill the store. Gavin was right: it's about to get busier. I pat my face dry and wash my hands. I fake a smile and walk up to the cash register.

"Hi, welcome in. What can I get you this morning?" I say as cheerfully as I can.

\*\*\*

The next three hours are tiresome. Trying to attempt small talk and sound happy. Every time the door dings, I look up in fear that it's the dark figure from out back. I've replayed the events over and over in my mind in between each customer. Maybe it was all in my head and it was just Lester being noisy. Whatever it was, it's got my tummy in knots and the extra shots of espresso I snuck throughout the morning when Gavin went to the back have me more jittery than usual. The sun I desperately wanted all morning is now blinding me in the face as I pour drink after drink. The door dings again. This time, it's Anna.

"Hey girl." Anna says as she walks cheerfully past the register and toward the backroom.

I nod in her direction, but I don't have the energy to say a word. I envy her in that moment. She doesn't have the past I have and most certainly didn't have the morning I had. She is oblivious to how cruel the world can be. I honestly hope she never has to experience what I've experienced in my short lifetime.

7:59 and Anna is ready on the floor. I watch her clock in. I'm ready to bust out of here. Normally I work four until nine with my classes starting at nine thirty. I've already decided I'm skipping my classes today. I pull my apron off and walk over to Anna.

"Gavin said I can go home early. I'm not feeling that well. I got a little dizzy this morning," I tell her.

"Oh, dang. Hangover?" Anna asks.

"No, but I'm going to get out of here before you-know-who changes his mind," I say as I point toward Gavin, who's chatting with some of our regulars out in the lobby.

"Oh, gotcha. Hope ya feel better," Anna says.

I sneak into the back, grab my things, and slip out the front door, unnoticed by Gavin.

The bus stop is a straight shot down the street, and even though the sun is out now, I study my surroundings carefully before each step. I find myself looking into every doorway as I pass by and looking behind me often.

A handful of people are waiting at the bus stop when I arrive. I lodge myself into the middle of the crowd. Safety in numbers, right? I pull a book out from my backpack. I always carry a book on my daily bus commutes; it keeps people from initiating small talk. It almost always works. Fingers crossed it works today. I should feel safe in the crowd, but I would rather not talk to anyone. I can't escape my fear of the dark figure in the shadows.

The bus pulls up and everyone piles in. I find an empty seat near the middle and keep my book open.

My apartment is only a few blocks away, but it takes around ten minutes with the frequent stops and its roundabout route to cover all areas. At this moment, I wish that I had brought my car to school with me. My cute little green VW Beetle. We pull up to the next stop and I keep my face buried in the book. I hear feet scurry by, and more chatter fills the bus. A body stops directly next to me.

"Is this seat taken?" A light, carefree voice asks.

"No," I respond coldly, without looking up.

The girl sits down and her perfectly sculpted thigh rests against mine. I continue to ignore her and stare into my book. She fidgets

in her seat and knocks my leg back and forth several times. I'm
annoyed, but the movement stirs up an intoxicating scent. A
huge change from the horrid smells of my morning. I can't help
but deeply inhale to gather more. A mix of lavender and rose
immediately calms me. I can't explain it, but I feel safe. Each time
she moves even the slightest inch, the scent stirs up and lingers in
the air. Is it her perfume or shampoo? I can't tell.

Her phone begins to ring and escalates with each trill. She jabs
me in the side with her hip and she shimmies for her phone that's
tucked tightly in her front right pocket.

"What do you want?" she shouts into the phone.

I'm intrigued now. I pretend to read but really, I'm eavesdropping.
I normally don't allow myself to get sucked into other people's
drama, but for a second it breaks me from my own reality.

She's bickering with the person on the other end. I lean in to
hear more, although I can't quite make out what the other person
is saying.

The girl next to me is quiet for a moment and then shouts
back, "It's not my fault you left your clothes all over the floor, and
then they ended up in the hallway."

She gives the caller a second to respond and then comes back
with, "No, you're such a slob, I can't take living with you another
minute." She takes a deep breath and then proceeds, "And
your dirty dishes, seriously. I saw things growing on a plate this
morning. Our room is not your science experiment."

More from the other end, and then, "No, you're the bitch." She
slams the phone shut and her body slumps down into her seat.

Her movement is dramatic and over the top.

I situate myself closer to the window to give her some space.
The girl lets out a deep sigh and slouches further into the seat,
sinking deeper with each breath she takes.

Wow, this girl is dramatic, however, I'm slightly entertained by her. Normally, this kind of need for attention would annoy me, but I can't help myself. She's clearly wanting someone to ask her about her phone call. I know my morning was way worse than her little phone call, but I'm compelled to ask her about it.

Never engage with people on the bus, Charlie. What are you doing? I almost regret the words as they leave my mouth. "Excuse me, I don't mean to intrude, but is everything OK?"

The girl in front of me turns around and gives me a dirty look. I'm sure she's thinking, "Why are you playing into this drama queen's need for attention?" Although, no one else seems to be phased by her, not even the cute guy across the aisle. Probably a frat guy who wouldn't mind giving her a little attention in hopes for a phone number in return. Nothing. I'm shocked. Maybe this is normal behavior for her, and they're used to it. After all, this isn't my normal time for the bus.

"Kind of you to ask," she says.

She peers up at me with the most beautiful ocean-blue eyes I've ever seen. I'm stunned by how pretty she is. She has a familiar smile.

I give her a grin and she continues. "Uh, my roommate is horrible. Just the worst. I really can't live with her anymore. An absolute slob, that's what she is. She left dirty dishes all over our dorm room. I woke up this morning and found a bowl of half-eaten mac and cheese on the floor. I nearly stepped in it. Who does that?"

Her arms flail around as she speaks—attempting to draw in more attention, I suspect.

"Sounds awful," I respond.

I study the girl as she continues. Her blonde hair rested heavy on her chest with about five perfectly placed curls spread throughout. Her face appears completely symmetrical with her lips glossed in a shimmery pink color. She is extremely pretty and very well put together for a college student from her extremely tight-fitting jeans and her champagne-pink sweater that appears to be cashmere all the way down to her UGG boots. Most people on the bus are wearing sneakers, sweats, and hoodies. I look down at my own attire and feel like a slob next to her. My work uniform of a white collared shirt and black pants doesn't create much excitement.

The girl jumps back into her story without skipping a beat. "She leaves piles of dirty clothes all over the floor. So ya know what I did this morning?"

I shake my head and she proceeds.

"I took them all, every single pile she left, and I tossed them out into the hall. Please don't think I'm crazy, I just couldn't take it anymore. She had to learn her lesson, ya know?"

"I don't have a roommate, so I guess I'm lucky," I say, not sure how to respond to her, this intriguing creature sitting next to me.

She rests her perfectly manicured hands down on her lap, giving them a break. I take notice of her Barbie pink nail polish that flawlessly coats each nail.

"You don't know how good you have it, girl," she says as she stares back at me.

I shift uncomfortably in my seat, this time not sure how to continue the conversation. I sit awkwardly, turned toward her. Luckily, she jumps right back into her story.

"So, after I toss all her stuff out, I marched down to the resident advisor's room and demand she move me to a different room. But apparently there's a long wait list. So now I'm screwed."

Her experience was typical for a freshman learning to live with complete strangers. A lot of my co-workers dished about their crazy roommates. One girl even peed on her roommate's bed when she was drunk because her roommate stole her leftover pizza out of the fridge. I'm so happy I don't have to deal with any of that kind of crap.

"Oh, and I'm Quinn by the way." She reaches out her hand to shake mine.

"I'm Charlie." I slowly extend my hand. She gives me a firm, strong handshake. I'm taken aback by her grip. I wasn't expecting that. This girl exudes confidence and is everything I'm not.

"What dorm do you live in?" Quinn shifts the conversation to me. I'm unprepared for this. People don't usually want to know about me.

"Um, I'm not in a dorm. I registered for classes late, and there was a waiting list for all the dorms, so my parents just found me an apartment about ten blocks from campus."

I didn't want to tell her all my parents could find with my last-minute change in schools was a two-bedroom apartment while she's stuck in a tiny room with a horrible roomie and I'm over here living in a large space all to myself. I'm happy to have the private space to process what happened with Jenny.

"Well, this is my stop," she says, interrupting my thoughts.

I reach into my backpack. I grab a scrap piece of paper and jot down my number. I hand it over to Quinn without even thinking about my actions.

"Here's my number if you ever want to hang out and escape your roomie," I say, and give her a kind smile.

Quinn gets up from her seat and shoves the paper in her pocket without even looking at it.

"Nice to meet you, Charlie. Thanks for your ear. I needed to get all that off my chest, although it doesn't change the fact that I have to head back to see the slob now," Quinn says.

She flips her hair back behind her shoulders and walks away. She turns back toward me and waves as she exits the bus.

***

The rest of the day, I thought about Quinn. She left an impression on me.

# CHAPTER 08

### Charlie
### August 2012

Its bumper-to-bumper traffic when I arrive in Portland. I forgot to plan for the lunch-hour rush.

Waves of emotion seep into my being as I slowly make my way up the 405. I'm afraid to hear what Quinn will say about the night I don't remember.

I need to know what caused her to leave.

What did I do that was so horrible?

Why didn't she call me all summer?

The anger and sadness on her face as she left haunts me.

Will the truth be too painful to hear? I don't think I'm ready for the truth.

So why am I here then?

A white SUV swerves in front of me, cutting me off and breaking my concentration. I slam on the brakes and swerve to change lanes for my exit.

So much dang traffic.

I'm cutting it close. It's nearly noon. I don't want to start off on the wrong foot with Quinn. I'm already on thin ice.

Downtown is buzzing as always. Keep Portland Weird is painted on one of the buildings, which totally sums up this eclectic area. For a normally mostly rainy town, it is surprisingly sunny today. Not a cloud in sight.

The hustle and bustle of the busy city is giving me little hope of finding street parking near the bookstore. Especially during lunch hour. I yank my steering wheel to the left at the first sign of a parking garage. I drive through the first level with no luck and round my way up to the second. A little white Subaru Impreza is pulling out of a stall near an exit sign. I'm relieved to find a space as the time is slipping by. I'm going to be late. Quinn is going to be mad.

A gaggle of homeless characters are congregated in the corner of the lot near my exit. I manually lock my door from the inside, avoiding the other option of a loud beep from my key fob.

Don't draw attention to yourself, Charlie.

Their backs remain turned away from me as I creep past them. The huddle breaks their stance once I'm almost past.

A tidal wave of cigarettes, urine, and whiskey opens up as the crowd breaks, hitting my nostrils hard with all three scents at once.

The familiarity stirs up an unwanted memory.

The day in the alley years ago.

Goosebumps run up and down my arms and legs.

I hold in my breath and run down the first flight of stairs. One of the crude characters follows behind me. I don't turn around.

Charlie, you're overreacting. This person isn't going to harm you. Lester didn't harm you.

But the other thing that day wanted to. I think.

A hoarse voice startles me. He's right behind me. Scents of ashy cigarettes waft past me.

"Can you spare a dollar?" The hoarse voice hisses.

I ignore him and keep moving faster.

What is wrong with me? Just give him a damn dollar. He's harmless. I'm being irrational right now.

My heart's pounding in my chest, and tingles run down into my fingertips.

"I know you can spare a dollar," he says and follows me down the next flight of stairs. "Come on now, little girl, I know you can afford it. Just give me a dollar."

I don't entertain him and keep my head down and finish the last level of stairs.

He stops to cough and catches his breath.

"Bitch," he hollers at me as I exit the garage. He doesn't follow me. Thank God.

I bend down to catch my breath. I'm breathing heavily. I close my eyes for only a brief moment and Jenny flashes across the backs of my eyelids.

No, not now.

I push my eyes shut so hard I feel my eyelashes brush against my cheeks. When I open them, everything is normal and Jenny is gone. Horns honking, traffic flowing, and people rushing by.

I push all the dark thoughts to the tiny little box in my mind. I wrap them back up. I suck in a couple of deep breaths and walk in the direction of the bookstore.

Today is about Quinn and me. Nothing else. Just us.

# CHAPTER 09

### Charlie
### August 2012

I'm officially late.

Why are there so many entryways into this massive store? We didn't pick a place to meet inside when we spoke yesterday.

We didn't discuss much of anything, really.

I grab my phone and text Quinn.

*I'm here. Where are you?*

I wait a few minutes with no response.

I may as well get a head start on finding a book. Quinn's normal impatience won't allow me much time inside. I jolt up the stairs, taking two steps at a time. Signs point me to the used-book level. I'm greeted by the distinctive smell of old musty paper. It fills the entire level. If I could bottle this smell up, I would. There is something to be said about a book that has lasted through time to be passed down repeatedly. One owner after another enjoying a story and escaping into a world that is not their own. I can't help but feel instantly better.

A copy of Agatha Christie's *Death on the Nile* is staring me in the face. I reach for it and give it a hearty sniff, hoping no one is watching, but at the same time, how could they judge me? It's a perfectly reasonable thing to do with an old book. I ponder how many people have owned this novel that came out in 1937. I'm sure it's a reprint, but I don't dare look at the date. I don't want to ruin the illusion. Either way, the curled edges and beat-up spine give evidence that it has had multiple owners.

I smile, feeling like my old self for just a second. A time before everything went wrong. A time when my life was simpler, and I was just a book nerd and Aunt Jenny was still here. I need this book. I hold it tight in my arms like my little security blanket and take it to the counter to purchase it.

While I'm at the register, I hear Quinn's voice from behind me. I let the cashier ring me up, but my focus is all on Quinn. I watch over my shoulder. I finish paying for my book and step aside, keeping Quinn in my view.

She's with a guy.

Of course, she is.

She's probably been in here all of five minutes and manages to find someone to give her attention. She is in her usual flirty stance, with her left foot turned up and her right hand resting on his shoulder with her body pushed into his. A flirtatious laugh echoes from above. I'm sure Quinn is enjoying the attention that she is getting right now. I knew she was an attention seeker from the first second I met her on the bus all those years ago. Nothing has changed, except her confidence grew more and more over time. Anytime she encounters someone attractive, she stops what she's doing and ignores everyone around her, including me. She sucks up the attention like a little monster.

Our friendship is complicated.

The guy follows her down the steps like a little puppy dog. Quinn brushes past me, completely ignoring my presence. Another flirty high-pitch giggle comes from Quinn as the guy poses for a photo with her. I guarantee her phone is filled with pictures of forgettable men. She says goodbye to Mr. Random and finally turns her attention to me.

"There you are. I've been all over this place looking for you," she says condescendingly as she struts back in my direction.

She looks perfect as always, dressed in a cute little faded denim romper and strappy fashion sandals. Silver bangle bracelets line her right arm. She's perfectly tanned with no evidence of tan lines. Her full blonde hair bounces with each effortless step she takes.

How does she manage to be so perfect all the time?

Quinn studies me up and down as she approaches. I didn't put much effort into getting ready this morning. Her right brow furrows, and her full lips turn into a disapproving pout. I can tell she's not pleased with my appearance, but she doesn't comment.

"Did you get my text?" I ask.

"No, sorry, didn't see it," Quinn says as she picks up her phone, stares at it, and then shrugs. "I see you got yourself a little book. Does that mean you're ready to go?"

"Yah, I'm good to go," I respond, holding my book tight against my chest.

The store is becoming increasingly busy, and people are bumping into us left and right.

"Gosh, watch where you're going, dude," Quinn says to a guy that walked right through the two of us. "Rude! Let's get out of here," and she waves me toward the exit.

We walk out a different exit than the one I came through. I'm a little turned around, gazing up at street signs to get my bearings. Quinn's pace is faster than mine, as always. I'm constantly lagging behind her. I've always assumed it's her long, toned legs. Quinn jogs nearly every morning, except on mornings when we partied the night before. I preferred the extra time in bed, but not Quinn. Quinn doesn't like wasting the day. Carpe diem, she always says.

"So, what's the plan?" I ask Quinn while taking longer strides to keep up with her pace.

Quinn slows down as we approach a crosswalk. She shifts her entire body toward me and wraps me in her arms in a tight embrace and says, "First off, it's nice to see you. I've missed you." I can't help but let my heart leap for joy, and a sense of relief fills my body.

"Quinn, I've missed you more than you can imagine," I whisper into her ear as our embrace lingers. Her hair blows along my face and stirs up her lavender calmness that I've grown so used to.

The crosswalk beeps, and she pulls away from me and drags me across the street with her.

"Clearly, you've missed me too, and my clothes. Have you been dressing like that all summer?" Quinn asks, waving her hand the length of my body.

I turn my head down and frown. For a brief moment, our embrace was perfect and just what I needed. I crave those little moments. Now here she is; critical Quinn is back. She takes more pride in my looks than I do, and she knows that. Did she really expect me to keep up without her guidance? She should know better.

Quinn frowns back at me. "so you took everything I taught you and tossed it out the window the second I, um, left . . ." She hangs on the last word. She doesn't want to continue. She's not ready for that conversation just yet, and neither am I.

"So, the plan is?" I press her to proceed and ignore her question.

"So, I thought it would be fun to get a hotel downtown. There is a free concert and beer festival tomorrow I thought we could go to. Have a little bit of fun like old times," Quinn says excitedly.

"Sure, that sounds nice. Although, I wish you would have told me what the plan was, so I could've packed accordingly. I didn't know what you had in mind, so I just threw together a quick little overnight bag in case we ended up spending the night. I didn't bring anything Quinn-approved," I say with a slight laugh to lighten the mood.

"Charlie, your Converse sneakers and cut-off jean shorts will not do. I know you too well, so I brought a few extra things with me. You can change when we get to the hotel," Quinn says in her usual condescending manner.

"Oh, I thought you just said everything is tomorrow," I say, confused.

"It is, but we still have the entire day ahead of us, and you want to look a little nicer. Don't you?" Quinn presses me.

Guiltily I say, "I guess I do, then." A fake smile and a nod end her interrogation.

"Hey, let's go grab our bags and meet back at the hotel. I'm sure they have a valet if you want to move your car. I will text you the address. It's just a block away, I think," Quinn says.

"OK. I think I will leave my car in the parking garage I'm currently in. It has overnight parking and probably costs the same, and I won't have to tip the valet."

"Whatever. See ya in a few." She blows me a friendly kiss and disappears down the street.

# CHAPTER 10

### *Charlie*
### *October 2008*

Last week I asked Gavin to move me to the afternoon shift. I lied and told him I joined a study group that my professor suggested to me, and it just so happened to start at eight in the morning. I couldn't do the four till nine shift anymore; I didn't want to quit but I couldn't bear the quiet, dark mornings after what happened.

Luckily Anna was looking for more hours, so I suggested she take the four to noon shift and make it a full eight hours. She recently dropped one of her classes because she was failing to the point of no return and only had night classes left, so my plan worked perfectly. Gavin was hiring extra afternoon help, so I snuck into that shift and Gavin didn't have to hire anyone. It was a win-win for everyone.

I clock out at 6 p.m. on the dot. I'm enjoying my new time slot and I get to work with people more my age. The assistant manager, Tony, is more fun than Gavin, and the other afternoon employees, James, Ella, and Matt work hard and mostly keep to themselves. We are all too busy to make small talk and the time flies by most days.

Matt likes to sneak a drag from his cigarette as often as possible, so he always volunteers to take out the trash. I haven't had to go out back once in the whole first week of my new schedule. Not once. It's been a huge relief. I haven't seen Lester or the terrifying, unexplained dark figure since.

I grab my phone and backpack from my work locker and dash outside. The street is busy, and the weather is nice for October. College kids are hanging out, soaking up the warm weather, and enjoying their Friday night. Tomorrow is a home game for the football team. I haven't been to one yet, but I do know this town gets nuts over football. Everyone is wearing black and gold and having a good time. All the restaurants and bars are packed, with the patio seating overflowing. Everyone is ready to party, and I'm ready to go home and relax. I suck at being a college student.

I make my way to the bus stop and pull my phone from my backpack. A missed phone call and voicemail appear. It's an Oregon number. I wonder who that could be?

I dial my voicemail and I'm surprised by the voice on the other end.

"Hey, it's Quinn from last week on the bus. Remember me? You gave me your number. So, here's the deal: my roomie is driving me insane, and I need to escape my dorm room for the night. Wondering if you were free and wanted to hang out. You mentioned you lived alone. Maybe pizza, beer, and a movie night? Sorry, I just invited myself to your home. Well, anyway, call me back if you want to hang. Also, are you from Oregon? I noticed the prefix when I called you. I'm from Portland! Anyway, call me." Quinn's voice is light as she speaks, excited, cheery.

Is this real? Maybe it's a prank. Does the pretty girl from the bus actually want to hang out with me? I can't debate this issue because I am in need of a human interaction from anyone at this point and if it's a joke, I really have nothing to lose.

I click on her number and hit call before I chicken out. Quinn answers on the first ring. "Hello."

"Hey, Quinn, this is Charlie. I got your voicemail." I attempt to sound cool and casual, but I'm sure I'm coming off as desperate.

"Hey girl, didn't know if you would call me back. Sorry for the long rambling message." Quinn laughs. "So, wanna hang tonight?" she says, sounding confident I'm going to say yes.

I pipe up and raise my voice to match her tone. " Yah, cool, what do you want to do?"

"Well, since you said you have a place all to yourself, I thought I could come over and we could chill and watch a movie. Maybe order a pizza and I can swing by the gas station and pick up some beer."

Beer? She can't be 21.

"Sounds like a plan," I reply, attempting to sound cool. I don't want her to second-guess calling me and figure me for a dull disappointment.

"What time works for you? The sooner the better for me. The slob is on a rampage, I'm about to lose my shit over here." Quinn says with a light laugh.

"I'm heading home from work. Just waiting for the bus right now. I need a quick shower. You can let yourself in if I don't answer. I will leave it unlocked for you. Just promise you're not a serial killer." I say and try to mimic her light, carefree laugh.

"OK, great! I will get the beer and then head over, and I promise I won't pull a Norman Bates shower scene on ya! Text me your address." Quinn is quick on her feet. I like that about her.

I laugh at her Psycho reference. Maybe we have the same taste in old movies. "OK, see ya soon."

"See ya!" Quinn says and hangs up.

I can't help but smile as I tuck my phone back into my backpack. The bus pulls up on perfect cue.

*** 

As I rush off the bus and run up the stairs to my apartment, I evaluate my need to clean. A few dirty dishes sit in the sink, but other than that, my apartment doesn't need much attention.

I rush through my shower and get dressed quickly as I was very trusting with my offering to let Quinn into my house. I should have been more careful with my words to a total stranger.

Nearly an hour passes as I sit and wait for Quinn to arrive. Maybe it is all just a cruel joke. I thought she'd be here by now. I start analyzing my apartment in case my new friend does actually arrive. I'm slightly embarrassed by how little I've done with the place. I have the basics as far as furniture goes, and it's all secondhand. I bought my couch off the guy who lived here last. He was moving out as I was moving in. We literally crossed paths on the stairs. I don't even think the landlord planned to clean, even though he was very clear about the massive fines I would incur if I didn't leave everything better than I inherited it. The previous tenant couldn't fit the couch in his moving truck, so he asked if he could leave it behind. I was happy to accept because it saved me a trip to the store and a lot of money. My parents couldn't make the trip out here with the little notice I gave them when I switched colleges at the last minute. They found me this apartment online and signed the lease for me. I ensured them I would be OK and could handle everything on my own. The rest of my stuff came from a thrift store down the street. I don't have a single thing hanging on the kitchen or living-room walls. My bedroom is a little nicer. I have a few family photos hung up in there. I keep the ones with Jenny tucked away in my nightstand. I like to think I'm keeping her safe.

My heavy head bobs down and startles me, and I realize I've been dozing off. I check my phone and another forty-five minutes have passed. I've been duped. I'm just a joke. Why would a girl like that want to be friends with me?

I get up to call it a night when a little rap on my door restores my faith.

I'm not a joke. She actually came. "Hello, Charlie," Quinn says outside my door.

"Come in—it's open," I say a little too excitedly.

Pull it back, Charlie. Control your excitement. Attempt to act cool.

Quinn opens the door and struts inside my apartment and slams a six-pack of beer onto my secondhand kitchen table.

I can't help but notice Quinn's appearance. She looks like she's ready to go out instead of a night in of pizza and beer. I'm not even sure if she has room in those clothes for pizza and beer.

Quinn's tight jeans and even tighter cream-colored sweater fit her body like a glove. Her breasts sit perkily under her top. Her blonde locks are styled as perfect as the day I met her. Nothing is out of place. Not one hair, not one smudge of makeup. I can't find anything wrong with this beautiful girl. What will she gain from being friends with me?

I gaze down at my own appearance and I suddenly feel sick. I didn't try at all. My yoga pants, fuzzy slippers, and a pullover sweatshirt hardly scream "be my friend." I've never cared about my appearance before and I'm a little disturbed that I find myself caring now. My mom and Jenny spent years trying to get me to care, but I ignored all their attempts.

"I've got beer!" Quinn says in a high-pitch voice. Almost singing the words, snapping me out of my evaluation of her, she pulls a bottle from the pack and twists the top off and hands it to me. She continues her effortless strut throughout my kitchen, looking and checking out every corner.

"Are you twenty-one?" I ask.

My question brings Quinn back to the table. She chuckles and responds, "I got some guy outside the Quick-N-Go Mart to buy it for me."

I've never been friends with someone so bold before.

She seems pretty proud of her accomplishment. Although I assume it wasn't really an accomplishment for Quinn at all; I figure this is normal for her, and given her appearance and her effortless charm, any guy or girl for that matter would be inclined to do so.

"Impressed?" she asks

"Um, yah. So, you just asked a stranger to buy you beer and he did?" I question.

"Yep, it's easy. Haven't you ever tried that before? How did you and your friends get your beer in high school?"

"I didn't really drink in high school, and I've only been to one party since I got here. This is my first real beer," I awkwardly admit to Quinn.

Now I know she is going to leave. I'm such a dork compared to her. She is so cool and I desperately want to keep her here.

I'm relieved when she says, "Well, welcome to college, Charlie. Cheers, my friend." Quinn holds up her beer for me to toast with her. I do as I'm asked and take a swig. A sour taste washes over my tongue, making my taste buds perk up. I choke it down.

OK, maybe she's cool with me.

"We need to break you into the college life, girl," Quinn says, pleased with me, like I'm her new project.

"Quaint place you got here, Charlie. Could use a little decor, though, don't you think?" Quinn is a little judgy, but I let it slide. I need a friend, even if she's a little condescending. I shake it off as a personality trait. Maybe she doesn't realize how she is coming across. I don't really care though; I want to be her friend.

"I haven't really gotten around to that yet. I've been busy," I reply.

"Well, good thing you've got me now. I can help you decorate, and we can get this pad looking like the college apartment it should be," Quinn says, inserting herself effortlessly into my life.

She gives herself a tour of the rest of my apartment. I hear her opening doors, but I don't follow her. I'm not sure how to act. I don't want to follow her around, but it is my apartment. I'm already exhausted from playing host and I haven't really done a thing. All the self-doubt and questioning is so tiring, plus the couple of sips of beer have made me feel groggy and dizzy. A feeling that is completely new to me. Quinn seems pretty self-sufficient, so I let her do as she pleases.

"So, you have an empty bedroom, huh?" Quinn shouts down the hallway.

I don't respond and let her continue to check out my bathroom and my bedroom.

She makes her way back to the kitchen, grabs her beer from the table, and plops herself down onto the couch.

Boy, she sure knows how to make herself comfortable.

"So, your phone number . . . Oregon?" Quinn questions.

"Yep, Bend, born and raised. You said you're from Portland?"

"Born and raised too. Too funny that out of all the people

here, I sit next to someone from my own damn state. We'll cheer to Oregon and new friendships," Quinn says as she raises her beer to toast me.

She reaches over for the remote on my end table, turns the TV on, and surfs the channels until she finds a movie that satisfies her.

"Oh, I love this movie—*10 Things I Hate About You*. Charlie, have you ever seen it?" Quinn asks.

"Me and my aunt . . ." I trail off. I'm not ready to share that with Quinn just yet.

"Huh, what, Charlie?" Quinn asks.

"Um, Yes. Good movie. Should I order pizza? Pizza Palace OK with you?" I ask Quinn.

"Only if we get Taco Pizza," she responds.

"It's the only thing I ever order from there," I say, satisfied with my recommendation and excited by how many things we already have in common.

"Charlie, I think we are going to get along wonderfully," Quinn says.

*** 

I wake to a dull throb in my temples, and my mouth is dry and parched. I stretch my arms out and I frown as I shake my head in confusion. My body shifts uncomfortably, and I realize I'm not in my bed, but I'm on the couch. I don't recall much after the pizza arrived and I don't remember Quinn leaving.

I hear students outside yelling, "Go Hawks!" I check the time: 8 a.m. Oh crap, game day. Sounds like the tailgating and partying are off to a crazy start already. There will be no peace and quiet for me today. This town turns into one big party on game days. Wafts of what I can only imagine to be sizzling beef on a grill flow into my slightly ajar window. I want to vomit. I've never felt so horrible. I scratch my head to gain clarity but fail miserably.

I search the room for clues and find the culprit immediately. Six empty beer bottles line my TV stand. I wonder how many of those I drank. I honestly can't recall.

I drag myself to the bathroom, passing a half-eaten open box of pizza lying in the middle of the floor. The stink of old pizza mixes with the beef from outside and I barely make it to the toilet. Everything from yesterday comes up.

With my head buried in the toilet I hear, "Lightweight," from down the hall.

Is Quinn still in my apartment?

I clean myself up and slowly make my way into my bedroom.

Quinn is sprawled across my bed.

"Good morning, sunshine," Quinn says.

"Morning. I didn't realize you were still here," I respond.

"I was too buzzed to walk home alone, so you said I could take your bed, don't you remember?" Quinn says convincingly.

"I must have had too much to drink. I don't remember much from last night," I admit.

Quinn wraps my blanket tighter around her. "You're fun when you let loose, Charlie. You're a little uptight when you're sober. Drunk Charlie is way more fun. Hey, want to rally and join the tailgate outside?"

"Nah, I think last night was enough. Not doing that great today." I rub my aching head.

"Suit yourself. Mind if I use your bathroom to freshen up. I'm going to join the party outside," Quinn says as she leaps from my bed, as if she didn't have a single beer last night.

"OK, I will join you," I say, fearing that I won't see her again if I don't play along.

"Great, just what I was hoping you'd say," Quinn says, pleased.

# CHAPTER 11

## Charlie
## August 2012

Quinn texts me the address just as I pull my overnight bag from my car. She was right; it looks like it's only about a block away. I'm thankful the homeless crowd from earlier has moved on. I wanted to tell Quinn to come with me for safety and sanity, but I knew that would mean explaining my unexplainable fear to her. She would say I'm overreacting, which I'm sure I am.

Another text from Quinn comes through as I make my way out to the street toward the hotel.

> *I checked us in. Just come up to the room. 802. I splurged! Top-floor suite.*

A suite? What is she thinking?

Typical Quinn. She can never wait for me. I hope she doesn't think I'm planning on chipping in. I would be OK with a motel, but not Quinn; she has to have the best. I can't help but think, here we go again. I know I let her walk all over me and she can be overbearing sometimes, but the truth is I have missed her and feel like part of me has been absent over the last three months.

I locate the address Quinn texted. The old brick building is weathered on the outside, but a fancy awning classes the building up. It's not your typical hotel, but rather a fancy boutique establishment that screams "downtown Portland" and "different."

"Good afternoon," a man with a blue blazer greets me and holds the door open.

"Hello." I politely nod as I walk through the door.

Inside the lobby, a beautiful silver chandelier hangs in the entryway and shines above the modern, posh furniture, creating an upscale atmosphere—a drastic contrast from the exterior. I wonder how many old buildings I've walked by, not knowing what gems lay inside.

I bypass the reservations desk and head straight for the elevator. A sign points toward the hotel bar, which is just a straight shot down the hall from the elevators.

I make a mental note. For later, perhaps?

It's barely the afternoon and laughter, chatter, and music erupt from the direction of the bar. The idea of a little bit of fun sounds great about now.

Just one little drink. Quinn can wait.

No. Charlie. Keep on track. Don't piss Quinn off.

Instead, I call the elevator and wait for the doors to open.

My phone vibrates, and it's Quinn again.

*Hurry up, slowpoke. Get up here—I'm waiting.*

Wow. She can be so dang impatient.

The top floor has only a few rooms. I imagine they are all

larger suites. I walk down to the end of the hallway and knock on
Room 802. I stare at the ugly pale-blue carpet, thinking it doesn't
fit the rest of the hotel decor.

Quinn answers the door and greets me with an impatient grin.
"Charlie, I've aged days waiting for you."

"How did you get here so fast? I swear I came straight here.
Elevator took a bit, but that's it," I respond.

"Eh, whatever, I'm over it. Come look at this view," Quinn says
as she leads me into our suite.

We walk through two large rooms. The first one has two king-size
beds, a TV, and two dressers. The second room has a little office-cum-
living area with a chair, couch, and an even bigger TV. Along the wall,
a minibar and tiny fridge with a pricing sheet sit on top a black counter
next to a microwave. Art deco paintings hang on every wall.

"Look at our cute little balcony," Quinn says, and she leads me
outside. "Isn't this amazing, Charlie?"

It wasn't the tallest building downtown by any means, but it did
have a nice view of the city.

"Quinn, it's great, but we don't need a room this nice. Isn't this
a little too lavish? A shower and a bed is all we really need."

"Oh boo, Charlie. I knew you would say that and that's why
I had you just meet me here. It's just easier if it's already said
and done with. Nothing you can do about it now," Quinn says
in her usual I'm-right-you're-wrong manner. She rolls her eyes.
"There's nothing wrong with lavish and enjoying yourself a little.
You should try to relax. What do you say we unpack our things
and head out for a late lunch? I'm starving."

I only brought a few things, so I sit back on one of the king-sized
beds and watch her unpack. Quinn tosses me a little spaghetti
strap purple tank top and a pair of jeans from her suitcase. "Wear
that," Quinn demands.

I obey her and excuse myself to the bathroom. I should've known better and prepared. I've had too much on my mind since I last saw Quinn that I've almost forgotten how overbearing she can be. Since the first time I hung out with her, I knew she liked things a certain way. She never goes out without looking perfect and that also goes for the people around her. I'm no exception. She always expects a certain level of preparedness and is easily irritated when things don't go her way. And yet, I was sucked into Quinn's world. I was mesmerized by her and the way she carried herself, so confident, so put together. Her controlling and demanding side is something I overlook to be friends with someone like her. I get to be a different person when I'm with Quinn. I needed a friend badly when I met Quinn and I fell for her; not in a romantic way, but in an intriguing, needy way.

Quinn bangs on the bathroom door, barely giving me a chance to slip my clothes off. "Charlie, are you done changing yet? I still have to fix your makeup and I'm getting hungrier by the second."

I quickly dress and open the door. Quinn storms in with her makeup bag in one hand and a flat iron in the other. "OK, let's take a look at what I'm working with here. Looks like all my hard work went down the drain. Maintenance, Charlie, it's called maintenance. It's like a car—you have to keep up on things or it's all going to go to shit."

Quinn abruptly walks out of the room and comes back, rolling a chair from the office setup. "Sit—this might take a while."

I listen to her and take a seat. It's not worth the argument.

Quinn doesn't skip a beat and immediately dives into everything wrong with me. I'm used to it, so I just let her talk.

"Charlie, these eyebrows, have you not plucked since May?"

"I don't remember, Quinn. I haven't had much going on lately. No need to, I guess. I've just been lounging around in my room,

surfing the internet for jobs. Hardly a reason to put in an effort."
Sometimes I do put on a little mascara, but I don't even bother to
tell her that. No point. It won't be good enough.

"So, you haven't found a job yet? I know this sounds crazy,
but if you apply for jobs all dressed up and ready to succeed, you
will. If you apply for jobs in your pj's, you won't. I know it's all
online but trust me it will make a difference. You will feel more
confident, and it will show."

I know Quinn is probably right, but my resumé and education
should speak for itself. But I know we live in a superficial world,
and I am more convinced that is the case the longer I have
remained friends with Quinn. She gets so much more out of life,
and I know a lot has to do with her looks. Jenny would easily get
things too. I want to try, I really do. The intention is there, but
then I just don't follow through. I can't explain it.

Quinn gives me an appalled look and grabs my hands. "Oh my
gosh, Charlie, your nails. Did you get hungry and couldn't wait
for lunch? Your nails aren't food, missy." Quinn hands me a nail
file. "Here, file these while I fix the mess that you've made of your
hair. Mind if I trim you up? The lob style only works if you keep
up with it. Remember, maintenance, Charlie. I will drill that into
your pretty little head by the end of the day."

"Sure, go ahead," I say.

Once I'm done filing my nails and Quinn gives my unruly locks
a trim. She tosses me a bottle of pale-pink nail polish. "Paint your
nails, please. I can't look at those little nubs all night without any
color on them."

Quinn only uses OPI. The cost of one of those small bottles
is higher than an hour's pay, but Quinn insists it's worth it. I
secretly love reading the creative names they come up with for
their nail polish.

The bottle Quinn tossed me is called "Getting Nadi On My Honeymoon." I giggle as I read the name. Quinn ignores me.

I once had a blue called "Can't find my Czechbook." It made me laugh each time I used it. Some were a little naughty, like a teal color Quinn gave me for Christmas one year called "Is that a Spear in your pocket?" I can't even recall the last time I painted my nails. I only put one coat on and wait for them to dry as Quinn adds the final touches of makeup.

"Charlie, honey, you know your lips are too thin to go without a good lip liner," Quinn tells me as she's holding my chin in her hands, concentrating on lining my mouth with the signature red she's assigned as my color. Quinn breaks occasionally to primp her own face and hair. She applies a clear lip gloss to her lips and a red lipstick to mine.

Quinn brushes a little bit of color over my cheeks, and it reminds me of the one time she told me I had good cheekbones. She never repeated it, but I always held on to that one feature she thought was maybe just a little bit better than hers.

She grabs an eyelash curler from her bag and asks, "Charlie, remember when you picked one of these up for the first time, and asked me what it was?"

We both laugh in unison. I remember Quinn looking at me like I was a martian. "What girl from planet Earth doesn't know what one of those is?" she had said to me.

"Yah, you were such a little clueless bookworm when I met you," Quinn says now.

"Hey, I'm still a bookworm and proud of it," I say, confirming my status.

That is the truth. I was pretty clueless before I met Quinn. Jenny tried to help me, but I never gave her the time of day with that kind of stuff. She eventually gave up. Before meeting Quinn,

I never wore makeup, I dressed very casually, my hairstyle was nonexistent. I just didn't care. Those things weren't that important to me. I'm not sure they're important to me now, but I continue to let Quinn play Barbie doll with me, finishing off her magic with her eye-shadow pallet. Quinn beams back, pleased with her work, and spins the chair around so I can look in the mirror.

I look like the life has been restored to my body. My eyes have a twinkle. My hair is smoothed out with zero flyaways. Somehow Quinn managed to even create a little shine in my dull hair. My lips appear fuller, and my face is perfectly covered in foundation, hiding all blemishes.

I'm nearly unrecognizable. "Quinn, you did it again."

I look pretty.

# CHAPTER 12

### Charlie
### August 2012

The afternoon is slipping away. That's what happens when Quinn and I are together. Quinn puts too much effort into everything, and I find my days floating by waiting for her. It's OK though. It usually ends up being worth it, and today I feel pretty, so I guess it's worth our time. I haven't felt like this all summer.

Quinn presses me to do things I would never do if I didn't have her as a friend. She opens doors for me that would normally never open. I stay friends with Quinn for the rush I feel when I'm with her. I know I put up with some crap, but truth is, it's easy to be friends with Quinn. She makes the plans, she dolls me up, and I go along for the ride.

As per Quinn's usual style, she finds us a cute little bistro down the street from our hotel. The hostess leads us through two brick archways and down a couple of steps where she seats us at a quiet little table for two. The tan walls and minimalistic artwork paired with smooth jazz creates a calm ambiance. It's not quite dinnertime, so the place is empty. It's the perfect setting for Quinn to finally bring up what happened the night I don't remember. Losing Quinn after that night was one of the saddest things I've had to endure, with the exception of Jenny, of course. Now sitting across from Quinn, I see that she is calm, and her features are soft. I don't see an ounce of anger across her face. Maybe she just let go of what set her off that night, but Quinn isn't known for letting things go.

Quinn did say she wanted to talk when she called yesterday but has yet to bring it up. I'm dying to know, but I'm also afraid of the truth. If it was something catty Quinn would've brought it up already.

Quinn loves to call me out on my wrongdoings, so it must be bad if she doesn't even want to talk about it.

"Charlie, I have to ask you something serious," Quinn says as she reaches out for my hands. She stares me dead in the eye. Her soft features turn stern.

Oh, this is it. Yes, I can handle whatever she wants to ask me.

Quinn's holding my hands tight, and I flinch, ready for what is about to come my way. I close my eyes, preparing myself to hear what awful thing I did.

"Charlie."

"Yes," I say as my heart falls to my stomach.

"I can't do this all on my own. I'm going to need a little help from you," Quinn says as she leans in closer.

"Huh?"

"Shall we split the surf and turf?" Quinn pauses and waits for my reaction.

"What? Surf and turf? Seriously. I thought you were about to talk about something serious."

"Ha, you should've seen your face. What on earth did you

think I was going to ask you?" Quinn laughs.

This is it, Charlie. Just ask her. Perfect opportunity. Pull off the band-aid. You got this.

I stutter as I spit the words out. The words I've been afraid to say. "Why did you leave me? Quinn, what did I do?" I turn my head down. I'm not sure I can look her in the eye.

"Oh, Charlie, that's not dinner talk." She puts her finger up to her lips and hushes me. "We can talk about that later. Let's order a bottle of cabernet sauvignon, shall we? Go all out. We need to celebrate the fact that we are together again." And with those words Quinn already has her arm in the air, flagging down a waiter. She didn't give me a chance to refute her idea and didn't even give our poor waiter a chance to come to us first.

A good-looking young man with wavy sandy-blonde hair responds to Quinn's request and makes his way over to our table. A huge grin appears across his face as he gets closer to us. He locks eye contact with Quinn from halfway across the room and doesn't break her gaze.

Quinn doesn't give the waiter a chance to speak and goes straight into her Quinn charm. "Hey, doll, can we get a bottle of cab for the table?"

He smiles, unaware that he is about to be sucked up into Quinn's tidal wave. "Sure thing, we have a Columbia Valley cab with notes of . . ."

Quinn holds up her hand. Palm facing out to stop him before he gets a chance to continue.

"I want you to pick out whatever bottle of cab you think I would like. Surprise me. What do you think a girl like me would enjoy?"

I watch Quinn twirl her fingers around her hair as she studies him. Her body is facing him, like an open invitation.

The waiter is practically drooling. I'm tempted to give him

my napkin to wipe his face or prop his chin back up. None of this surprises me. I find it a little annoying now. I used to enjoy watching her because I knew I could never have the nerve to act like that. I found it amusing. I at least benefited from the freebies that usually came with her flirting.

"Place an order for the surf and turf too with an extra plate. Now, go be a dear and fetch me that wine. I'm dying of thirst." She shoos the man away. Poor thing.

"Wow, that guy was practically drooling all over you," I say to Quinn.

"I know, how cute was that? I wrapped him around my fingers before he even got a chance to speak."

"Speaking of guys, how's Nash?"

I'm surprised Quinn hasn't said a word about Nash yet. Nash was the one guy Quinn consistently let back into her life. Every other guy was disposable, but not Nash. He was the first guy I saw Quinn keep around for more than one date, and the first guy Quinn met when we became friends. Nash has been around for a while now. He was obsessed with Quinn, as most guys are, but what made Nash so special was, he could handle Quinn's need for attention without getting jealous. He knew where he stood with her and could handle her off-and-on switch. I think he assumed he would get the girl in the end and eventually she would give up and settle for being his one and only.

"Uh, Charlie, you know how Nash was getting. He never wanted to accept that our relationship was just a booty call. Nash was getting too clingy, asking too many questions about our relationship and our future. And I was all like, dude, you were fun, but college is over and so is our little playtime."

"Quinn, so what's wrong with someone adoring you and wanting to be with you. Isn't that what every girl really wants after all? You had your fun in college. Couldn't you just settle down with someone who understands and accepts how you are?"

This is the most pushback or reality check I've ever given Quinn. I can't help but feel protective of Nash. He's been through the ringer with her and I'm sure she wasn't kind when she let him down.

"How I am? What's that supposed to mean?" Quinn says defensively.

"Look at our waiter, for example. Nash got that this was part of your thing and he accepted it. You're a flirt and you need attention. You and Nash were dating, Quinn. I wouldn't call him just a booty call."

"Nope, just a booty call," Quinn says with a snooty tone.

"A booty call that lasted three and a half years, Quinn," I taunt back.

"Anyways, Nash wanted me to follow him to grad school in Chicago and I had to put a stop to it. His neediness was unattractive, and I just couldn't have him latching onto me like that. I felt trapped and I had to get out. That's how I ended up in Seattle. My dad knew a guy that worked at a marketing firm and they were hiring summer interns. I figured why the hell not. If it didn't work out, I was at least closer to home and could call it a failure, and it was a failure but something good came out of it. In between bagel and coffee duty, I met the most amazing guy."

I give her a smug look. Leave it to Quinn to find some hunk to latch herself onto as she is running away from one.

"I know, I know, I said I didn't want Nash because he wanted more, but Charlie, with Asher its different. He's different. He helps me be a better person."

I highly doubt that, but hope it's true.

Quinn glows and smiles from ear to ear. "So, Asher was brought in to audit the firm I was working for. I took his coffee order one day when he was in the conference room with the CEO and other executives. After his meeting he found me and asked me on a date, and ever since then we were hooked on each other. Get this, Asher is from right here in Portland and was just in Seattle for six weeks. I met him the first day he was in town, so we spent practically the entire summer together. He had to fly down to San Francisco two weeks ago and he just got back to Portland. So, I haven't seen him in two whole weeks, and I actually miss him."

"Wow, Quinn, I'm kinda impressed that you're taking this seriously." I give Quinn a genuine smile.

"Charlie, you will just melt when you see him. He is so handsome. Slightly over six foot, golden-brown hair—the kind you can run your fingers through, and it falls back into place perfectly. He has a distinctively sculpted jawline, like that of a model. Oh, and he has a six pack, just saying. Really, the perfect man." Quinn giddily laughs. "I miss him and can't wait to see him again tomorrow."

"Huh, tomorrow? Is he coming with us?" I question.

"Yep, I can't wait for you to meet him." Quinn says.

"Oh, so it's going to be me, you, and Asher tomorrow, then?" I find myself tapping my fingers on the table, annoyed that I have to share Quinn tomorrow. I'm not excited about meeting this guy. I know she's saying the right things for once, but I also know he won't last. Not worth my time getting to know him. It's our time together, they both live here and she can see him when I leave.

But, I know it is no use arguing.

Quinn ignores my question, with her new distraction walking in our direction. Waiter Boy confidently walks up to our table, wine bottle in hand with the label presented toward Quinn. "Here is the bottle I chose for you, pretty lady. I didn't catch your name though," he says smoothly.

"That's because I didn't tell you. You had to earn it, and by the looks of that bottle, I'd say you did. It's Quinn," she says flirtatiously.

"Well, Quinn, pleasure to meet you. I'm Ted," he says.

"Well, Ted, what does this wine say about me?" Quinn asks.

Her little show confirms exactly what I thought. Asher hasn't changed her at all.

Ted's tone is low and playful. "I picked this one for you because it's a bold, full-bodied wine with hints of vanilla and ends each sip with a sweet cherry bite that leaves your mouth wanting more."

I roll my eyes. Poor fool. Quinn is not interested in you, just what she can get from you. I want to scream, "You're being used, Ted." But instead, I sit back in my chair and watch the show play on.

Ted reaches across the table for Quinn's wine glass. He brushes her shoulder doing so. Quinn smiles back at him.

"Give this a try, Quinn," he says, handing her a full glass of wine. "Did I get you right?"

Quinn takes a sip and purses her perfectly glossed lips together before answering, "It's perfect, Ted, you nailed it. Now will you be a dear and go check on my dinner."

\*\*\*

A few hours, some more flirting with Ted, and a bottle of wine later resulted in a partially comped meal and Ted's phone number on our copy of the receipt.

"I got it. It's only $40," Quinn offers.

She slides some cash into the tab and doesn't pull out the receipt with Ted's phone number. Instead, she leaves it exactly where she found it. Poor guy. The queen of flirting had played him.

Quinn's mood changes as soon as we leave the restaurant. For some reason, she seems more agitated now. "Do you mind if we just go back to the hotel and crash? The wine made me a little tired. I think I'm ready to call it a night if you are?" Quinn asks.

I don't argue. "It's been an exhausting day with the long drive, so that's fine by me too."

"Perfect," Quinn says.

Quinn walks with a swift pace for someone who is tired. I catch her pulling her phone from her purse several times and checking it.

"What's going on? Are you expecting a call? You didn't end up sneaking Ted your phone number, did you?" I question her.

"No, just checking the time. Nothing to worry about. Can you walk any faster? I'm ready to get cozy and relax for the evening." Quinn says, and we walk in silence the rest of the way to the hotel.

***

An hour later, Quinn emerges from the bathroom, her nighttime routine complete. Just then, Quinn's phone rings. Her eyes jump around the room, searching for her cellphone.

She leaps over the bed, scrambling to get to it. She locates it on her pillow, and once she has it in her hand, she silences the call. Quinn gives me an annoyed look but doesn't explain the call or her reaction.

Up until that moment, I thought maybe my suspicion was unfounded and in my imagination, but now I'm convinced something is going on. She's being secretive, but about what?

I stay sitting on my bed with my book in my lap. I pretend to ignore her, but I'm watching her out of the corner of my eye. She stares anxiously at her phone without looking up, presumably waiting for what I assumed was a voicemail or an incoming text from her mysterious caller. Quinn had been acting odd about her phone since we left the restaurant.

Seconds later, her face loses color, and her features harden. I don't think she's aware that I'm watching her. Yet, she appears to be cautious with her actions. She gets up slowly, trying to avoid my attention. She doesn't say a word and makes a direct path to the balcony with her phone in hand.

I should turn away, except I don't.

I can't help myself.

I keep watching.

Quinn is keeping at least one secret from me. She won't tell me what happened the night I don't remember, so who knows what else is going on with her. I haven't seen or heard from her in three months and she's making me wait to talk about that night.

Why are we waiting? What are you waiting for?

Quinn always does what Quinn wants to do and doesn't ever feel the need to explain herself, but this is different. Her actions are out of character.

I continue to watch her cautiously, avoiding her detection.

She shuts the sliding glass door behind her, eliminating my ability to eavesdrop. She hits a few buttons on her phone and waits a moment, then pushes a few more.

I watch her pace the tiny balcony with her phone pressed tightly against her head. It appears she is yelling, but her actions don't appear to express anger, as her brows furrow and the expression of concern spreads across her face instead. Everything about this situation is odd and out of character for Quinn. She loves having a good fight in front of me and craves the attention I give her afterwards.

Suddenly, she pulls the phone from her ear and tucks it back into her pocket. Her shoulders fall and her head drops. I honestly don't know what to think.

Who could have caused that reaction? Was it Asher? I hoped not—I wasn't feeling up to dealing with a heartbroken Quinn tonight. Which would be a first. No one breaks Quinn's heart. She doesn't let them.

I decide it would be best if I take a shower. I can hide out in there for a while to let Quinn cool down and decide what and how much she wants to share with me.

The shower's water is almost too hot, but I don't change it. I need to feel something other than confusion, even if it's a little painful. The scolding water flushes down my back, causing my muscles to spasm and tighten. I'm so confused by all the unknown.

I want answers from Quinn.

I want answers from myself.

I want to know why I ended up at Liam's house twice this week.

I want to know why Quinn invited me here if she has no intention of filling me in on what I did.

What is going on with her?

I want to shout.

I want to scream.

My best friend is sitting in the next room, yet I can't bring myself to ask the questions to get the answers I really need.

Maybe I'm scared of the truth.

# CHAPTER 13

### Charlie
### August 2012

I wake to the sound of a door closing. It takes a moment before I put the pieces together.

Quinn's bed is empty.

I immediately jump out of my bed and run to the door. I peer down the hallway with no sight of her. I rush back inside and grab my phone. It's 2 a.m. Where the heck has she gone at this hour?

Before I text her, I check her dresser. Her car keys are still here, but her purse and phone are gone. She didn't text me or leave me a note. It's definitely possible she's sneaking out for a booty call, but without her keys? Maybe Asher is picking her up. But why 2 a.m. and why wait until I'm asleep? If it's a booty call, she would flaunt it. Something is wrong if she's trying to be sneaky. She doesn't want me to know what's going on. I've never seen Quinn act like this before.

I can't help but think this has something to do with the phone call she got last night. What could Quinn possibly be hiding from me?

I text her even though I have a feeling she would rather I didn't know she is gone.

*Hey, everything OK? Where did you go?*

I wait a few minutes with no response, so I text her one more time.

*Where are you? I'm worried!*

Still no response.
What are you hiding, Quinn?

# CHAPTER 14

*Charlie*
*August 2012*

The click of the electric key-card lock startles me awake.

My eyes bolt open.

It didn't take me long to remember that Quinn disappeared last night. I must have dozed off waiting for her. I flip on a dim light next to my bed and check my phone.

No messages, and it's five in the morning. Clearly, she didn't care that I was worried, or she would've responded.

I leap from my bed to confront her.

I catch Quinn quietly tiptoeing into the room. I cut her off at the bottom of her bed and catch her off guard. "Geez, Charlie, what are you doing?" she yells at me.

"No, Quinn, the question is what are *you* doing? Where were you? You didn't respond to my messages. I've spent all night worrying about you!" I scream at her.

Quinn avoids eye contact and keeps her head down as she speaks. "I'm fine. I couldn't sleep, so I went down to the lobby."

She chews on her lip.

She's lying.

I notice her disheveled hair and she looks like a mess. Quinn never looks like a mess. She steps around me. "Everything is fine. Can you just go back to bed? I'm tired." She tosses her purse on the dresser and crawls into her bed.

I continue to press her. "Quinn, what's going on?"

She turns her body toward the wall and pulls the covers over her head. Her messy long blonde hair sweeps along her pillow.

"Charlie, just let it be," Quinn mumbles from under her blanket.

I stumble back to my bed and do as she asked.

Quinn is quiet.

I let it go. I could press her, but I know the outcome will be the same. I lie silent in my bed with my thoughts running rampant.

About ten minutes later, soft sobs emerge from Quinn's bed. I don't bother to ask if she's OK. I know she won't tell me the truth. She is not doing this for my attention. Something is really going on with her.

I close my eyes. I want to sleep, but images of Jenny smiling and laughing engulf my memories yet again. Then like clockwork, the shadowy reality veils over all the joy, and the darkness sets back in.

Rapids waves of crimson rush against my eyelids.

Jenny screams.

# CHAPTER 15

## Charlie
## October 2008

"Are you serious? I can't have another drink. I'm still working off the ones from last night," I say as Quinn hands me a full cup of foaming beer.

We are outside my apartment complex on the front lawn with about thirty other students. It's barely 9 a.m. and everyone is acting like it's normal to drink at this hour. Jenny always told me stories of her college parties, but never in my wildest dreams could I have imagined they looked like this, nor could I imagine Jenny behaving like all these people.

"You said you would rally with me. This is what rallying is Charlie. Welcome to college," Quinn responds.

Quinn takes a huge gulp of her beer and runs down the lawn to a group of guys grilling hot dogs and brats. Not exactly what I would call breakfast food.

She comes back with two hot dogs in hand and passes me one.

"Here, eat this. You need something in your belly, then I

promise you will feel up to partying. You don't want to miss out on this rite of passage. This is what college kids do," Quinn says.

I take a few bites of the hot dog and I feel my tummy filling up. The food is just what I need. Maybe Quinn does know what she's talking about.

"Hey, let's make our way down the street. The guy grilling down there told me about a frat party that is supposed to be absolutely crazy fun. Come on, Charlie, let's go. I've never been to a frat party before, and I'm positive you've never been either. Please. Please can we go?" Quinn begs me.

I hesitate, my heart pounds inside my chest, and I'm feeling a little anxious about all the new things I've done in the past twenty-four hours. This is a lot for me to take in.

Quinn's face is unreadable as I try to gauge my response. If I say no, will I ever see her again? If I say yes, will I regret it later? Both scenarios bounce back and forth like a game of Ping-Pong in my brain. I weigh each decision and finally settle on my answer.

Uncertainty coats my words. "Sure, let's do it."

I stuff the last bite of the hot dog in my mouth, taking my time chewing and comparing myself to Quinn, who woke up as perfect-looking as she was last night. I threw myself together this morning. Quinn offered to fix up my hair, but I didn't feel comfortable enough to let her. I want to run back inside and fix myself up. Next time I will accept her help—if there is a next time. I feel inadequate next to her.

I can feel her eyes on me now. Could it be my imagination?

"Relax, Charlie. Do you trust me?" Quinn asks.

What kind of question is that? I've only known her for less than a day. She is a total stranger to me, but yet somehow, I do trust her. Maybe it's the early-morning beer or the uncontrolled atmosphere that's making her my safety net, but it is something.

Quinn doesn't wait for me to respond. "Come on," she says as she flings her arm around me, yanking me across the lawn. "This is going to be so much fun. I promise."

I give in and let her lead me to the party. We walk arm in arm, giggling the entire way, like we've been friends forever.

\*\*\*

I'm shocked as we stand on the sidewalk in front of the frat house. A giant old redbrick building with Greek letters stands before us. I feel like I'm in a movie. I've walked down this street before, but never on game day. Everything is amplified today. Over the top. I'm nervous but I'm also very excited.

I've managed to miss every game day since I moved here. I heard things got crazy, so I stayed home. It seemed easier that way, and it's not like I've had friends to go and party with. If my high-school friends could see me now, they would think I've lost my mind. This was not the Charlie Faye they knew—or the Charlie Faye I knew, for that matter.

This is not me, but on some level, I want it to be.

I'm scared. I'm cautious, but I have Quinn to lead the way.

The yard is long and leaves coat the browning grass. The smell of fall is in the air. I still can't believe I'm at a college party, and a frat party to boot. Kegs of beer line the fence as far as the yard is long.

We cut through a group of guys decked out in black and gold face paint playing bags on the lawn. They scream and shout and encourage each other to chug. More than one intoxicated person bumps into us as we make our way to the center of the party.

"We need to find the person selling the cups," Quinn says, interrupting my thoughts.

"This is absolutely nuts. I thought these kinds of parties only happen in movies," I admit.

Quinn laughs at my remarks. "Oh, sweet Charlie, we are going to have so much fun together. I'm going to corrupt the shit out of you."

We finally make our way down keg row to a guy standing next to the first barrel, wearing a gold T-shirt with black painted lettering stating the pricing for his precious red Solo cups.

CUPS:
$5 for Girls
$10 for Guys

I reach in my pocket to pull out a five-dollar bill. Quinn shoots me a piercing look; a look I haven't seen from her before. She confidently flips her hair back and struts over to the guy in the T-shirt. I can't help but stare in amazement. This must be how she got the beer last night. She leans over and kisses the guy on the cheek as her hand slowly grabs two cups from his stack. She skips back toward me with two cups in hand, with a huge ear to ear grin.

Quinn offers me one of the cups. "Like taking candy from a baby," Quinn says, proud of herself.

"OK, that was pretty impressive," I admit.

We both giggle and run over to an unattended keg. Quinn fills our cups up.

"Sure you're up for this? I want you to have fun, but I don't want to pressure you into something you don't want to do," Quinn says with sincerity.

"I just can't believe I'm at a party like this. I think I'm OK. Thanks for encouraging me to come."

I smile and take my first sip of beer and as the foam hits my lips a cop car drives down the street. I quickly lower my cup, and Quinn laughs. "Charlie, they aren't going to do anything. They would be busting the entire city if they really cared. We just can't leave the property with an open container."

Quinn was right, the cops drive by like the entire party is nonexistent.

"OK, I guess I'm feeling more comfortable now. I still can't believe I'm drinking this early in the day. Quinn, you're one dangerous girl, aren't you?"

I watch another group of gorgeous guys tossing footballs while running the length of the yard, bobbing in and out of the crowd. One of them catches my attention and the ball. His tousled chestnut brown hair sparks my interest first. Then he flashes us a huge grin as he smashes the ball down in excitement. There is something about his look that makes me feel like he doesn't fit in here. Sure, he's included and playing ball with these guys, but something is out of place. I can't put my finger on it, and maybe that's why I am drawn to him. We are both outsiders, at least that's the story I make up for him in my mind.

Quinn catches me ogling over Mr. Tousled Hair. "Should we go over and say hi?"

I get the feeling she knows I will say no. Is she teasing me?

I can feel my face blushing. "Oh, no, Quinn. I couldn't." I want to tell Quinn about Liam and how I will never trust another guy as long as I live. I've been hurt worse than she could ever imagine. I'm damaged, but I'm not ready to tell her that story. It would mean I would have to tell her about Jenny too, and I'm not capable of saying those words out loud right now, or maybe ever.

I choke down a huge gulp of beer and with that I let go of the thoughts that were about to invade my headspace. I'm surprised

I'm able to wash them out of my mind. Nothing ever seems to work, but this beer has done the trick.

Quinn moves on from her teasing and we make a lap around the party. I'm in awe as I take in my new environment.

I'm stunned when I see a big-screen TV outside on the patio. Now I know I'm in a movie. Who does that? Massive amounts of extension cords run along the patio and back into the house.

"Hey everyone, it's kick-off time," a frat guy shouts to the crowd.

A couple of grills are fired up with burgers and brats going. Hordes of people start making their way to gather around the TV. A chant breaks out in the crowd, "Let's go, Hawkeyes, let's go." It's on repeat until the opening kick takes place.

"You want to watch?" Quinn asks.

"I'm not a football kinda girl. I'm OK if we keep walking around." I respond.

I couldn't care less about the game. I want to see what else this party has to offer. I am still feeling out of place, but the more I drink, the more my nerves let go. I'm starting to get used to the taste now too.

We walk around to the back of the house, where I spot two guys in lawn chairs on the roof next to a sound system. I assume they are the self-proclaimed DJs of the party. I had never seen anything quite like it.

"Who's ready to party?" They yell in unison out to the crowd of people below. Everyone screams and they turn the music up louder. People start dancing and singing. Quinn and I join in.

Hours, and many, many drinks later, Quinn and I are drunk, and I've witnessed her flirt with more men than I can now count on my fingers. Not once does she introduce me, but I don't really care. I'm just enjoying the entertainment of it all.

I'm dizzily sitting down on a lawn chair next to Quinn, wondering how long we've been sitting here.

Quinn shouts at me and tosses an empty cup in my direction to get my attention.

"Hey, I'll be right back," Quinn says, and she takes off down toward a large group of guys. I watch her whisper in one of their ears, and before I know it, Quinn is being hoisted upside down by two guys. One of the guys is Mr. Tousled Hair from earlier. He has one of his hands on Quinn's ankle and the other on her inner thigh.

Is she trying to make me jealous? My heart sinks. I'm sad for a moment. I didn't want Quinn to be that kind of girl.

Quinn is now in full keg-stand pose with the tap in her mouth. I watch her chug the beer as the crowd grows around her and starts chanting, "Chug, chug, chug." A guy off to the side of the keg is the timekeeper. He shouts, "One, two, three . . ."

When the count gets to thirty, Quinn taps the side of her leg, indicating she's had enough.

The guys put Quinn down. She wipes her face clean with the back of her hand, then wraps her arm around Mr. Tousled Hair and pulls him in for a kiss. He doesn't stop her.

OMG. She is that kind of girl. I have to look away. I feel a wave of anger rush over me.

When I turn around, Quinn's running back to me with a smile spreading from ear to ear.

"Did you see that?" Quinn questions.

"Yah, I saw, and then I saw you kissing the guy I was looking at earlier," I say sadly.

"I'm sorry—I didn't realize that was the guy from earlier. Don't be mad, Charlie. I truly didn't realize."

I can't tell if she's lying or honestly didn't know.

She pulls a ripped-up piece of paper from her pocket. His phone number and the name Nash is drunkenly written on it.

Wow, this girl moves fast.

Eventually, I'm too drunk to think about Quinn's possible betrayal. We drink the entire afternoon away.

We walk home, arms linked together like best friends. Quinn leans into me and says, "Hey, I think I should move into your extra bedroom. You cool with that?" Quinn asks nonchalantly.

I can't help myself and say, "Yes, perfect idea."

# CHAPTER 16

## Charlie
### August 2012

Daylight desperately attempts to bring life to our hotel room, although a dark cloud still lingers around our beds. I lie still, slightly groggy from the nightmares that ravaged my brain last night.

I can't bear to close my eyes again.

My chest stiffens and I know it's time to fold the darkness up in its tight little box and tuck it away before the images sneak into my consciousness.

I stretch, trying to shake the past week off and start fresh today.

I roll over on my side, now facing Quinn's bed. I'm relieved to see she didn't feel the need to sneak out again. Her long blonde hair hangs off the bed. She looks peaceful right now.

I slowly toss the blankets off and creep toward the bathroom, careful not to wake Quinn. She will need more than just a couple of hours of sleep to get through all she has planned today. I still can't help but wonder what last night was all about. I highly doubt I will get any answers today though, so I won't press her. An irritated Quinn is not a fun Quinn. I guess I will let her tell me when she's ready.

Today could be fun—A beer festival and live music. I don't remember the last time I did anything social.

Fresh start. New day.

I brush my teeth and get dressed and head down to the hotel restaurant.

I order pancakes, bacon, and a large coffee. I take my time eating because I know Quinn will still be sound asleep for at least a few more hours. The waiter makes small talk with me, but it's nothing like the attention Quinn would get. I will be paying full price for my breakfast.

*** 

Back in the room, I'm surprised to hear the shower going. Quinn's normally a morning person, but I assumed she would want more than a few hours of sleep. I guess I'm wrong.

I grab my book and have a seat on the balcony. Outside, the fresh air kisses my face. I can finally breathe. I take a deep inhale and slowly exhale, trying to center myself. I've never had much luck with meditation, but I try, nevertheless. I close my eyes and let the sun heat up my face as I stay focused on my breathing.

Inhale.

Exhale.

The traffic buzzes in the street below, soothing me into a calm relaxation. I hear the whooshing of the cars passing by and chatter from the busy commuters. Calmness covers my entire being; for a brief moment, I actually feel at peace.

Today will be a good day.

\*\*\*

Quinn finds me on the balcony an hour later. "I'm ready to go," she says.

I frown in frustration. "I still have to get ready."

"Oh, Charlie, you always make us late," Quinn says with annoyance in her voice.

Well, I wouldn't make us late if you didn't always hog the bathroom for hours. I don't say this, of course.

"Well. I didn't want to wake you since you came in so late last night. I figured you would be pleased with the extra sleep, so I snuck downstairs for some breakfast. I didn't want to be noisy."

"Ugh, let's get you put together quickly. You showered last night, so it looks like it can be a dry shampoo kind of day. Asher is going to be here in thirty minutes."

"Thirty minutes, Quinn. I had no idea we were on a timeline. You didn't tell me."

Why does she always do this to me? She never fills me in until the last possible second.

"Well, I'm telling you now." Quinn tosses me a little yellow sundress and a pair of white sandals. "Here, wear this," and pushes me into the bathroom. I don't argue and let Quinn do my hair and makeup.

It doesn't look like my friend is going to divulge any details of her whereabouts last night.

Deep breath in. Deep breath out. Today can still be a good day.

\*\*\*

The familiar sun from earlier greets me as we wait for Asher outside our hotel. Quinn appears uneasy, a drastic change from moments earlier. I've known her for a long time and have never seen her like this.

"There he is," Quinn says as she points at a sleek and ostentatious silver Mercedes-Benz S-Class Coupé.

I try to get a glimpse of him as I walk around the car, but his windows are tinted, making it hard to get a good look. I slip into the back seat, and then Quinn slides into the front. By the looks of his car, I'm guessing he has money—another thing my friend is drawn to.

Quinn scowls at Asher as she gets situated with her seatbelt. I thought it would be a good time for her to introduce me, but she doesn't. Asher is cold and doesn't offer an introduction himself, either. I'm sure Quinn told him I was coming, but for all this dude knows, I'm a random stranger who hopped into his car.

I clear my throat—a reminder for Quinn. She stays silent.

I follow Quinn's lead and stay quiet, too. She was so excited to introduce me yesterday but now I'm feeling like things changed. Maybe it was Asher on the phone last night and she snuck out to have it out with him. But why did he agree to come today if they're fighting? Is she hoping to make up with him? I don't feel comfortable being the third wheel if that's the case.

The scowl continues from Quinn, and Asher reciprocates. Quinn says something under her breath. I can't hear what she says, although Asher's own frown in return leads me to believe it wasn't positive.

"Great weather," I say from the back seat, with no comment from either party in the front seat.

Clearly, being given front-row tickets to an argument already in progress, although the view is not great.

I take the silence as a good time to get a read on Asher. His brown hair has a touch of natural curl toward the tip. My side position from the back seat doesn't allow the best view, but I can see his pronounced jaw and high cheekbones. His skin is flawless and freshly shaven. His eyes are piercing blue, just like Quinn's, showcasing their natural twinkle. He is beautiful. Exactly Quinn's type and exactly how she described him, except she left out the part about him being a cold jerk. I wonder if this relationship has run its course. If things were different, I imagine the two of them being a power couple who command a room wherever they go, everyone stopping, staring, and envying them. Although as of right now I doubt that will happen, and I kind of hope it doesn't because Asher has not made a good impression with me.

Luckily, it's just a quick five-minute drive down to Waterfront Park where the festival is held. I'm half tempted to ask him to pull the car over and walk. But I don't. I keep quiet because Quinn keeps quiet. I don't need another reason for her to be annoyed with me.

We approach a drop-off area and Asher pulls up to let us out. I'm relieved because I don't think I could be with these two in a car much longer. At least he has the kindness to drop us off.

"I will meet you back here in a few minutes. Wait for me, please. I'm going to park the car," Asher says to Quinn.

Quinn and I exit the car, but not before she tosses her champagne-pink cardigan sweater on the seat behind her.

She pops her head back and I hear her tell Asher, "I'm sorry." Asher responds, "Why did you lie?"

Quinn doesn't respond to Asher's accusations, and I pretend I haven't heard a thing.

What is Quinn lying about? I knew something was going on.

I attempt to break the awkwardness. "Chivalry isn't dead," I say.

I don't dare ask what's going on because it is even more clear now that Quinn doesn't care to fill me in.

"I suppose not." Quinn frowns and the light that twinkled in her eyes earlier seems to have disappeared. Was she like this all day yesterday and I didn't notice?

Crowds of people walk by us. Rows of tents and stages line the park along the river.

"This must be a big event." My attempt at small talk is lacking.

Quinn checks her phone a few times and shrugs her shoulders.

Wow, this is going to be a long day. At that moment I decide once we get inside the festival, I might go solo. I doubt these two will even know I'm gone.

Quinn's irritation continues as Asher rejoins us.

"Parking was nuts. I said screw it when I saw a sign at a parking garage that said $30 event parking. I figured it's early enough in the day that people would still try to get free or cheaper parking, and I scored a good spot right away. It was worth it," Asher says.

Is this Asher's way of trying to sound cool and impress us that he's willing to pay thirty bucks for parking? Dude, calm down.

Once we finally get through the line and inside the festival, I say to Quinn, "Hey I'm going to check things out. Looks like you and Asher might need some alone time to figure things out. I'm not sure what's going on here, but you guys don't look happy."

I boldly walk away before Quinn has a chance to refute my claim. I'm sure that just pissed her off, but I'm so over it I don't really care. I'm not going to let Quinn get in the way of my good day.

*** 

My mood elevates the further I walk into the festival. Hundreds of people smiling and laughing and having a good time. I can't help but smile and enjoy the contagious environment. Quinn and

Asher can figure their shit out, and Quinn, with or without Asher, can join me later. I'm going to have some fun.

I walk into a long white tent. One tap after another line the entire perimeter. I walk up to the first one. A *Double IPA* it says on the sign. I don't know much about beer, and most of my beer drinking took place at college parties with a red Solo cup out of a keg of PBR or Bud. Not this fancy beer that's described as having "hints of grapefruit and lemon."

A grizzly of a man shouts toward me, "Want to give our double IPA a try?"

He looked like a typical guy from Portland. A step back in time to the nineties when grunge was popular.

"Sure, why not?" I hand the guy my money and sip the beer and head toward a stage that's gearing up for the first band.

"Check one, check one." A loud voice says into a microphone.

I wait with a crowd of people for the music to begin. The mic check and sound check continue, and I gaze around. No Quinn and Asher in sight. Perfect. Today is going to be a good day.

The band starts and they excite the crowd. Everyone takes a long stride toward the stage until we are all packed together like sardines. I'm in the middle of the crowd and ready to let loose and have a fun time. My beer is cold against my lips and its bitter taste has a bite that leaves my mouth watering and thirsty for more. I get why people love their beer so much in Oregon.

I'm drinking. I'm singing. I'm enjoying myself. But slowly I feel my mood shift with each swig of beer I take. My cup is almost empty.

As the band plays on, something cold and wet rushes down my back, all over Quinn's yellow dress.

I abruptly turn around to find a large beer-bellied man drunkenly singing, beer swishing out of his cup with each move he makes. I give him a dirty look and gulp down the last of my drink. I try to ignore him and move, but the crowd shifts with me and he's still behind me. Another swish of cold beer makes its way down my backside.

Last straw, buddy.

I'm angry. Not just at this beer-bellied slob, but at Quinn, and myself. I'm angry Jenny is gone. I'm angry at Liam. I'm angry.

So much for my good day.

I twist my body and before I know it my fist is diving into the round beer belly behind me. I gasp in horror at my actions. I've never done anything like that before. Luckily, the man is too drunk to be phased by my little punch. I take off, pushing my way through the crowd before he can even realize what just happened to him.

I'm back in the beer tent and stop to catch my breath. I'm scared by my actions but also exhilarated by them. That was the most freeing thing I've ever done. I smile.

I order two more beers to avoid the line later. With my double fist of beer, I decide to find a grassy knoll to sit on by the river. I sip and think.

The exhilaration is wearing off, and my confused sadness hits me again like a pile of bricks. One brick after another piling on top of me until I can't breathe.

I find myself going down the dark hole that I know I can't pull back from.

I feel like it was a mistake coming here. Quinn doesn't want to talk about the last night we were together, and now she doesn't want to talk about what happened with Asher or whoever she snuck out to see last night. I really can't take this anymore. Maybe our friendship has run its course and it's time for both of us to go our separate ways.

I'm keeping secrets from Quinn, too.

That's the first time I've admitted that.

I never told her about my aunt Jenny. Saying it would have made it real. No one knew me in college, and no one knew our story and the horrible circumstances around it. I had a fresh start in Iowa.

Quinn was a much welcomed distraction, and every time I wanted to tell her about Jenny, I couldn't get the words out. I tried but I could never actually get myself to say them.

I kept Jenny's memory tucked in my nightstand with all her pictures. If I didn't speak about her, then maybe she could still be alive, living in my parents' guest house like nothing happened. If I didn't speak those words to another human being, then I could hide the dark reality and pretend it didn't happen. I know it sounds crazy, but that's how I deal with it.

The nightmares were still there when I was in Iowa, but they were less frequent. It was so much easier to forget with Quinn and the extensive social schedule she kept us on.

That's why I thought I needed her again to distract me, to keep me busy. To keep me on track. But it's all backfiring now. I feel I'm spinning out of control.

I'm dizzy.

I'm drunk.

I'm ready to go back to the hotel.

I want to find Quinn and leave.

Now.

# CHAPTER 17

### Charlie
### August 2012

I stumble along the riverwalk, trying to control my balance, but I'm swaying. The hot midday sun makes it worse; my skin is heating up. I need to find Quinn. I don't feel well. I'm drunk.

Do they even care that they haven't seen me in hours? I'm the forgotten third wheel. They don't fucking care about me.

I jaggedly cut through the crowd, my steps long and exaggerated. My heart thumps in my chest, tapping against my ribs. Sweat beads down my back, washing away the spilled beer. The bass of the band reverberates through my body. It's too loud. I can't think. I need to find Quinn.

\*\*\*

I'm not sure how long I had been looking when I spot them near the restrooms. Finally.

My movements are not fast. I will my legs to go faster but they don't listen. I try to call out, "Hey guys, hey, wait up," but my words come out slurred. They don't even look in my direction.

Something is not right. Even through my drunken haze, I notice that something is off. I'm too far away to hear, but I stay put and observe. Are Quinn and Asher arguing? Both of their mouths are moving fast and in unison, not giving the other a chance to listen. Quinn is doing that thing with her arms when she is irate, flailing them around with each word she spews at Asher.

Asher reaches his hand toward Quinn's shoulder, but she pulls back. There's panic in her ocean-blue eyes. I'm not sure what to do, if anything. I feel the ground spinning below me.

Asher glares back with a disappointed look. He attempts again to touch her, and before his hand reaches her, Quinn screams, "I didn't lie. I don't understand what you mean." Her voice rises an entire octave. A crowd of people turn and stare.

"Quinn, stop. Let's talk about it," Asher demands, but Quinn is already in a full sprint toward the river.

I also run but stumble and hit the ground. I pick myself back up and yell, "Quinn, wait." She doesn't hear me, or if she does, she doesn't care. I look back over my shoulder and see Asher walking in the other direction.

Quinn's blonde locks bounce along her back as she jaunts down the riverwalk. I'm dizzy, lightheaded, and feel weak, but I proceed. God, I wish I didn't have the third beer. Or did I go back for more? I can't remember.

Quinn stops in the distance. I catch up and call out to her again. "Quinn, I'm coming, please wait." She turns when she hears my voice this time. I'm almost to her now.

But her eyes are cold as she stares in my direction. She's not pleased to see me.

I'm confused. I'm dizzy. I feel the ground moving, the world spinning. My vision is narrowing.

Everything goes black.

# CHAPTER 18

### Charlie
### August 2012

Chills rush through my body, and it thrusts in shock.

Where am I?

My eyes flutter and burn as I force them open. Nothing is coming into focus. Something cold makes its way down my forehead and pools in the corner of my eye. It stings.

My body feels heavy. Weighted.

I tell my arms to push me up, but they are weak and tremble as they attempt their task. Something scratches under my palms as I push my body up. My strength fails me, and my body slams back down to the hard, scratchy surface.

Where the hell am I? I'm frightened.

Where did Quinn go?

My head is pulsating. I feel like I've been hit with a baseball bat. Everything is spinning. I drift out of consciousness.

# CHAPTER 19

### Charlie
### August 2012

A shot of panic scares me awake. My body tingles and my head throbs. I still don't know where I am.

I rub my eyes and something sticky and wet transfers to my hand. I'm frozen with terror. I pull my hands away until they come into focus in front of my eyes. I study them, although my vision is blurred, I see red. My heart drops into my gut. That can't be blood . . . Why would it be blood?

Slowly, one memory shifts to the next, like a car running through the gears as it accelerates.

I remember Quinn and Asher fighting. Asher said Quinn lied. Quinn ran. I chased after her.

She saw me. Didn't she? I swear I remember her looking straight at me, but if she did, why isn't she here? We were down by the river. I shift my attention to study my surroundings. The little sliver of moonlight doesn't offer much help, but I'm sure I'm not anywhere near the river. It's outside, it's dark, but I know I'm not where I last saw Quinn.

Have I been moved? Did I walk here? What happened to me? Did I black out or did someone hurt me?

Think Charlie, think. What happened to you?

I can't tell if it's the effects of drinking or if it's my possible injury, but the throbbing in my head is intensifying, and hot flashes run through my body. I want fresh, cool air, but instead hot heavy humid air is all I'm presented with. I want to vomit. I need to get out of here. Wherever *here* is.

My legs don't want to move yet. They tingle and feel weak. I push my palms down and what I imagine are little pebbles sting my hands as I prop myself into a sitting pose and push myself alongside what appears to be a brick building. I don't seem to be on a busy street, and I haven't seen a soul since I woke up. No one even knows I'm here.

I press my back against the bricks, feeling the coolness against my skin. I feel my body temperature lowering back to normal. I'm more alert now. Tears rush down my cheeks. I'm so confused. Is this the same thing that happened to me outside Liam's house? This time Quinn was here. Why didn't she help me? At Liam's house I was all alone.

Time to get moving, Charlie. You can do it this time. Get up.

My legs shake and tremble as I slide up along the brick wall.

Stay calm. One step at a time.

I shuffle my feet forward through the pebbles; my foot kicks something up. I bend down and I feel lightheaded again, but I push through it. I retrieve the item and it's my purse. Oh, thank heavens.

I didn't even remember to check for my belongings. I quickly rummage through the contents and everything seems to be accounted for. So, I didn't get mugged, I guess.

Get it together, Charlie.

I pull my phone from my purse and dial Quinn. It rings and goes to voicemail. Strange.

I call several times and finally leave a voicemail on the final call.

"Hey, you've reached Quinn Sullivan, I'm not free to answer my phone, so please leave me a message, and if you're lucky, I will call you back." Quinn's tone is free and fun and not like the Quinn I just saw today with Asher.

"Quinn, where the hell are you? I saw you leave. Didn't you see me? I chased after you. I don't know where I am. Please call me back. I need help."

If Quinn gets that message, she has to call back. She will realize I'm in trouble and call me right away. Right?

I walk until I come to a well-lit street. It appears I was in an alley. No wonder no one saw me. Why was I there, though? I can't even see the riverwalk from my location. How did I get so far away from the festival?

I walk for a couple of blocks, confused and disoriented, before I stumble upon an open restaurant. Should I go in? I need a bathroom badly; I need to evaluate my appearance before I call a cab or continue my walk to the hotel, wherever that may be.

Eventually, I will be around more people and heavier traffic. I need to see what I'm dealing with.

I quickly strut inside with hopes of going unnoticed. A whiff of fried food and hamburger grease blasts me in the face as I pull the door open. The hostess chats up the bartender in the dark bar area. She doesn't even turn toward the sound of the door swishing open. I luck out again with the bathroom being just to the left of the entrance. I push through a large, heavy door—I don't even bother to look at the gender sign—and lock it behind me. I just need to be inside and hidden. It's a single restroom with a lock on the door. Perfect. Just what I need.

I walk toward the mirror and my heart falls into my gut again. I look worse than I imagined.

Streaks of dried blood run the length of my face, stained with my splotchy tears. I fill the sink up with water, reach over for a handful of paper towels, and begin to scrub my face until it's no longer red with blood but red with irritation instead.

Dark, dry blood cakes my hairline. I wipe it the best I can and use the soap from the dispenser, which smells like lemon, to clear the crusted-on bits. It looks like it's just a small gash. How did that little cut produce so much blood? I've done worse to myself and have bled less, that's for sure. I rush to evaluate my entire head but don't see any other gashes or lacerations, but I notice more blood streaks along the back of my arms. This can't all be my blood.

Just a tiny cut—it's not possible.

Did I hurt Quinn? This doesn't make sense. I couldn't have. I wouldn't have.

I grab my phone and call her again. No answer.

Why isn't she answering? She has no reason to be mad at me. Nothing is adding up right now. Do I go to the police? And tell them what? I'm drunk and I can't find my friend.

The police are useless in my opinion. They didn't believe me last time.

*Jenny.*

I need to get back to the hotel. Maybe she's sleeping. That's probably it. It's nearly eleven now.

I scrub the rest of the blood the best I can and flush the paper towels down the toilet. No evidence. I wipe the sink clean.

I'm dizzy but I have to keep it together.

I call for a cab before I leave the safety of the bathroom. I take one last glance in the mirror. My irritated, puffy red face stares back at me. My hairline wet but cleared of the blood. A small cut that's no longer bleeding hides under my hair. I did what I could.

I put my head down, hold my breath, and pray for the best.

The hostess, still flirting with the bartender, doesn't even flinch when I close the door behind me.

I find a grassy area off to the restaurant's side to sit and wait for my cab. I hope my cabbie doesn't think anything about me. I'm sure cab drivers see all sorts of things or couldn't care less what their passengers look like as long as they get paid. I continue to call Quinn over and over while I wait. Still no response.

A yellow cab pulls up.

"Hey, are you, Charlie?" the driver asks.

I smile and slip into the back seat.

***

I'm back at my hotel. A place I couldn't be happier to see. I run inside and rush through the lobby and into an empty elevator. I sprint down the hall and anxiously use my key card to open the hotel room, receiving an error light the first two times. Come on, come on. Finally the green light. I push the door open and I barely let the door close behind me and I'm hollering for my friend.

"Quinn!" I rush over to her bed.

It's empty.

I check the balcony and every corner of our suite. Quinn's not here.

I can't control my breathing. My chest tightens. I feel like I'm suffocating. I yank my dress down to my ankles until it's a little yellow pool at my feet. I fall down to the floor and sob between wheezes. I don't understand what's going on.

I crawl to the shower and turn the water to hot. It burns my skin. The hotter the better right now. I scrub my entire body until my skin feels raw. I close my eyes as I hold my face under the scolding water.

Visions of Jenny smiling wash over me, making me feel happy again, making me forget for just a minute.

The shower splutters hot and cold water, and the pressure fluctuates. I don't know how long I've been in the shower. I finally shut the water off, and as I dry myself, I replay what I remember.

Asher and Quinn fought. Quinn fled. I chased after her.

I may or may not have blacked out.

I don't know where Asher went.

Quinn isn't answering my calls.

I don't know if I hurt Quinn or if maybe Quinn hurt me.

I had more blood on me than I should have for my small cut.

I wrap myself in the white hotel robe and grab my phone and text Quinn a series of texts.

*I'm back at the hotel.*

*What happened to you?*

*Are you OK?*

*Are you with Asher?*

*Where are you?*

*Quinn, where the fuck are you?*

I wish I had Jenny to comfort me right now. If only things had been different. If only. . .

# PART TWO

2008

# CHAPTER 20

## Charlie
## January 2008

Tiny snowflakes slide down my window as I stare at the empty street below. There is not a single tire track in the fresh powder yet. The beautiful view outside my window should calm and relax me, but I'm anxious. Today marks the beginning of the end.

It is the first day of my last semester of high school. Just a few short months and everything will be different. I want to talk to someone about it, but no one is home. Jenny told me she's working late tonight and my parents . . . Well, who knows when they will be home. I have already called my friends, Zoey and Mike, and both of their parents said they were at club meetings. I forgot Zoey has French Club on Mondays and Mike has Sierra Society. My extracurriculars are lacking, but I've already been accepted to Oregon State University, so I don't really see the point in trying so hard anymore. I will keep my grades up and keep looking forward. That's all I need to do. Just a few short months. I can do this.

I'm going to miss my parents, but I will miss Aunt Jenny even more. Everything else I'm OK leaving behind, yet I can't help but feel anxious about it.

Ugh, hurry up someone, get home.

I gnaw on my fingernails, chewing them down to the quick. The metallic taste of blood causes me to pull back and finally stop. It's a habit I have to break.

The snow has picked up now, with larger snowflakes flying against the window. A loud, rattling noise takes my attention back down to the street as an old beat-up red car rounds the corner by our house.

Dang, get a new muffler.

I'm taken aback when the car stops directly in front of our house. That's odd—we aren't expecting anyone, and I don't recognize the vehicle. I stare out the window but stay slightly tucked behind my tan curtains, out of sight. A guy exits the beat-up car, cautiously leaving his door ajar. He puts his hand on his chin like he's thinking. Large snowflakes land atop his head. He reaches back into the car. A piece of paper appears in his hand.

I watch as he stares at the paper, then gazes at our house and back at the paper again. He runs his hand through his hair and scratches his head. He shrugs his shoulders and walks away from his car toward my house. I keep watching him from my window. I almost lose my breath when he comes into clearer view.

Wow. He's hot.

I don't think I've ever said that before about a real person. Sure, I've said that about movie stars, but no one in real life. This guy is hot, and he's coming toward my house.

Is he going to knock on my door? Who is this man?

I jump out from behind my curtains and rush into my bathroom. I run a brush through my messy hair.

I'm startled by my actions. This is not a normal reaction for me. The doorbell rings.

Oh my gosh, he's actually coming to this house. What on earth does he want?

I rush down the stairs while running the brush through my hair once more. The doorbell rings again. I toss the brush back toward the landing and hear it thump back down a couple of steps.

I'm in too much of a hurry to look back to see where it landed. I quickly glance down at my attire as I approach the doorway. I cringe at my oversized gray T-shirt and tiny little pajama shorts with little red hearts on them. Too late to turn around. Of all the things to be wearing to answer the door for the prettiest guy I've ever seen . . . He rings the doorbell a third time.

I swing the door open a little too enthusiastically. "Hello?" I greet the beautiful stranger.

Goosebumps line my bare legs as the cold wind and snow waft their way through the entryway and around my body.

The stranger flashes me a wide, confused grin. His right eyebrow rises up, and he scratches his head like he did outside earlier. I stare at him, waiting for him to get his words together. "Um, yes, um, I have an appointment with Dr. Jenny." The words come out as more of a question than a statement.

My aunt Jenny prefers that her patients call her "Dr. Jenny." She says it is more for their comfort than her own. I think it makes her sound unprofessional, but what do I know?

He stares at me, as if waiting for me . . . Oh, shoot, I forgot to speak. I was in my own head again. Boy, he's beautiful.

He stares at me awkwardly, and I can't help but gaze at him as he continues. "I don't think I'm in the right place, but I can't seem to find the correct address." This time he is more confident with his statement.

I'm speechless and completely stunned by his appearance. I realize I still haven't said anything besides hello. He probably thinks I'm so dumb, but still, he proceeds. "The address Dr. Jenny gave me is 435 1/2 Lemmings Way, but all I can find is 435. I'm sorry to bother you." He smiles as if he had done something wrong and wanted me to tell him it would be OK. He is like a cute little puppy.

Speak, Charlie, use your words.

I'm about to answer him, explain that my aunt's house is behind our home, but he continues to talk and talk, and his beautiful bright white smile has me in a trance. "Dr. Jenny told me it was behind a house or a small house next to a house. I really can't remember." He scratches his head again.

I continue to listen to him ramble about his confusion as I take in his features. He has light brown hair that hangs slightly over his left eye. I could get lost in these large brown eyes, and I can't help but stare at his insanely long eyelashes. I've never seen a man with eyes this gorgeous. His face is sun-kissed. But it's winter. Perhaps he is a snowboarder? My imagination runs wild about what he would look like under his black Patagonia coat.

He knocks me from my trance when he says, "Um, I'm sorry, this clearly isn't the right house."

I stare blankly at him and I try to speak, but his attractiveness makes me stutter.

"I, I, I, um, you do have the right place. Well, kind of. Dr. Jenny is my aunt, and she lives in the house behind ours. She usually tells people to park on the side street and walk down the alley."

"Oh," replies Mr. Handsome. "That was the one thing I forgot. I'm so sorry to bother you, but what is the best way to get there from here?"

I gleefully respond, "I probably shouldn't be doing this, but you can walk through the house, and I will take you out back."

He smiles graciously at me and replies, "I'm Liam, by the way. I just have sleeping issues, that's why I'm seeing your aunt."

The puppy-dog gaze is back again. Oh, he has me. My knees wobble a little as I grin at him and reply, "I'm Charlie, and I understand. I know she treats all types of people and disorders. Not that she tells me about her patients or anything."

I guide Liam through our house, then over across the yard and around to Jenny's front door.

"It was nice to meet you, Liam. Have a good session." I cringe as the last part comes out of my mouth. Why did I say that? Gosh, "Have a good session?" That sounded so corny.

I try to think quickly and act cute to redeem myself. "You should probably walk around to the street when you leave. I probably shouldn't have let you walk through our house—the other patients might get jealous."

Much better.

I smile a flirty smile, then prance away, remembering the short shorts I'm wearing, hoping Liam will turn to give me a second look.

Who am I?

I turn around once I get to our backdoor, and Liam is already inside Jenny's place.

My actions stun me. Is this what a crush feels like? This is not normal behavior for me, especially around boys, or should I say men, in Liam's case? I wonder how old he is. I desperately need to know everything about him.

# CHAPTER 21

## *Charlie*
## *January 2008*

It's a dreary winter day and the weather has me feeling tired and sluggish. I thought this semester would be a little more exciting as it's my last, but I'm back into my old routine: coffee for lunch to avoid the cafeteria. I drink more coffee than a hard-working adult, Mom says, but I look forward to my midday pick-me-ups. It also helps break up the monotony of my day and lets me escape my mundane high-school life, if even just for thirty minutes. I'm ready for college to start. I'm over high school. I don't care about sports or dances or any of the things normal girls my age care about. I don't gush over boys at lunch with my friends like other girls do.

Although, there is a guy I can't get out of my head.

Liam.

He's all I've been thinking about since he accidentally walked into my life last week. Yesterday, I caught myself daydreaming about him and nearly missed my entire class. Thankfully, I didn't get called on. I had to stay up late last night to reread all the chapters that were discussed. I didn't want to fail my test today because I couldn't get a stupid boy out of my head. If I had just paid attention like the good little student I usually am, I wouldn't be in this situation right now. Sluggish, tired, and feeling all giddy and weird inside.

Get it together Charlie, this isn't like you.

The line is unusually long at Coffee Loon today, and I keep to myself as it slowly inches forward.

The barista shouts out one name after another and then, to my surprise, I hear a name. His name.

"Liam. Medium Americano with room for cream."

I adjust my posture and wait anxiously to see if it's really him, if it's my Liam. I keep my eyes fixed on the pickup counter.

Please be him, oh please be him.

Oh, my gosh. It's really him.

My legs flounder below me. Oh, this has to be divine fate working its universal magic. I'm nervous and don't know how to react. Do I say something? Do I hope he sees me and remembers the awkward girl from his therapist's office? But why would he? He's way out of my league. I'm not even sure I'm in a "league" at all.

"Line's moving," a voice whispers behind me.

Oh crap, I forgot to move. Pay attention, Charlie, you're acting like a fool.

I don't want to miss my opportunity to talk to him, but it would be awkward if I get out of line now to approach him.

I have butterflies in my tummy as I watch him move over to the condiment bar. His unforgettable swooshy brown hair and gorgeous grin have me giddy inside. I watch as he picks up a carafe and pours cream into his drink. It looks like we have the same taste in beverages. Something we already have in common, except he has to ruin his with cream. I will ignore that little infraction.

Finally, my turn to order. "Medium Americano, no room," I say hastily, without giving the cashier the time to ask me what I want or exchange pleasantries. I promptly pay and step closer into his line of sight.

Please notice me. Please see me.

I quickly move over to the pickup counter.

He is now chatting with a guy by the condiments bar. Good, he's not leaving just yet.

The barista yells, "Medium Americano for Charlie."

I reach for my drink, and I see Liam shift his entire body when the barista shouts. Is he responding to my name? Did he hear "Charlie" and hope for it to be me? Maybe he couldn't get our encounter out of his head either. Maybe I'm dreaming. I pinch myself and a little tingle pricks my skin. I feel something. I'm not dreaming. This is real.

He says goodbye to his acquaintance and is now taking long strides in my direction. My knees quiver and I feel faint. His hair whooshes with each stride. Before I know it, he's standing directly in front of me. He's taller than I remembered. "Charlie, right?"

Oh my, he remembers my name. The butterflies multiply by a thousand.

I want to play coy and pretend he didn't leave an impression on me, but I giddily respond, "Yes, and you're Liam."

"Ah, you remember me," he says with a cocky smirk.

"How could I forget the lost little puppy at my house," I say.

Oh, my gosh, did I really just say that? I want the floor to open up beneath me . . .

He laughs. "Touché. To be fair, though, it's quite a confusing setup Jenny's got going on. Her office is tucked off the street and hard to see."

"Well, that's why you have to follow her directions and listen when she tells you to park in the alley," I say, confidently defending my aunt.

"Well, checkmate, Charlie. Hey, would you like to join me?" he asks and points toward the tables along the wall facing my school.

I don't tell him I only have ten minutes before I have to be in history class with the dreadfully dull Mr. Dennison, who has a unique skill to make the most exciting events in history sound incredibly mundane. Instead, I have a chance to sit and chat with Liam. I can't miss that opportunity. A guy, this beautiful guy, is giving me attention for the first time in my life. I can't pass this up. I have every intention to leave in five minutes and make the quick run back to school. But right now, I could spare five minutes for Liam.

Except Liam's a talker, and I don't account for my head-over-heels infatuation with him and my inability to walk away.

I listen to him as he spills out details of his life, like an open book. I don't know how we got into such a deep conversation all about him. I must have spaced out again while taking in all his beautiful features.

Oh, that smile. It has a hold on me. I lean in and listen to his every word.

"So, I'm attending community college, got a late start – that's why I'm a twenty-one-year-old still working toward my two-year degree. Took some time to backpack through Europe first. I stayed in hostels, just me, a backpack, and my trusty camera. I really want to be a photographer. Anyways, I met a lot of exciting and fun people. Crashed on a lot of their couches, but eventually I had to come back to the States and get the ball rolling with school. Plus, I had to help out with my niece."

I smile and Liam doesn't skip a beat. I wonder if he sees the drool dripping from my mouth and pooling on the table. I double-check my chin to make sure I'm not actually drooling.

Stay cool, Charlie.

I can't stop staring at him. This time he doesn't have a coat on, so I can see what I could only imagine before, and it's exactly how I pictured it. His long-sleeved blue polo shirt is bulging from his muscles, accentuating every line.

He's got this little vein that sticks out in his neck when he talks, and I can't stop staring at it.

"My brother-in-law died from cancer about six months ago. My sister's been lost without him, so I try to pick up the slack and help take care of Lily. My little Lily Pad. That's what I call her."

Oh, and he's sweet and loves his family. Mr. Perfect.

The bell rings across the street at my school. I check the time. Crap, crap, crap. History class is starting right now.

I could run across the street and slide into my seat before Mr. Dennison even realizes I'm late, but then I would miss out on getting to know Liam.

Screw it. I'm staying.

Whoa girl. This isn't like you. Maybe you should tell him you're in high school and only seventeen.

I quickly quiet my inner voice of caution.

"So, what kind of photography are you into?" I ask Liam, and shut down my thoughts of rational reasoning.

"Just about anything but I'm really passionate about nature scenes, like capturing the perfect light as it dances off the water, or the way the sun hits the mountains at the perfect time of the morning. That kind of stuff, ya know?"

"That sounds beautiful," I say

"Hey, Charlie, I gotta get going—Photo-editing class at two. Nice chatting with you today. Maybe we can bump into each other again tomorrow?" Liam says as he stands up and grabs his coat.

I smile. "I would love that."

I can't stop staring as he exits Coffee Loon.

I replay every detail of our conversation. I didn't realize it at the time, but Liam never asked me any questions. It was all about him and he's a talker. It's OK though, because I want to know everything about his life, and I learned a lot. It's probably best I don't tell him I'm missing class while I sit here and listen to his stories. I don't want to tell him I'm in high school until I have him roped in. He wouldn't have asked me to join him at his table if he didn't feel something for me, would he? I can't tell Jenny about this, even though I tell Jenny everything. I know it's wrong, he's so much older than I am and he's Jenny's patient, and yet . . .

I don't want Jenny to be disappointed in me.

# CHAPTER 22

### *Jenny*
### *February 2008*

I'm keeping secrets.

I know what I'm doing and I know it's wrong, but I can't control myself around him.

I let him into my life and now my bed. I've been sneaking around and it's thrilling. I love the way I feel when I'm with him. I can actually feel my heart skipping beats each time he touches me—like a teenager in love for the first time.

I haven't felt this level of excitement in a really long time. I've been too busy to allow myself this kind of fun. If I'm being honest with myself, it was the kiss that started it all. Sure, I was attracted to him, but I would never have acted on it alone. His confidence as he strutted across the room toward me. He knew I could be his. I don't think the thought even crossed his mind that I would say no. I never gave him the impression that I was into him, not once that I can recall. Maybe his self-assurance is the reason why I am even more attracted to him. And when his lips touched mine, I couldn't pull away. I should have, but I didn't. In that moment, I knew this kiss would change everything.

I broke the rules the second he was in front of me, and his bold, beautiful eyes met mine. I stared into them for what felt like forever. I should've said something before it went too far.

His soft, sweet lips pressed hard against mine, and I kissed him back.

I can't get that unforgettable night out of my head.

I've already let it happen, so what would be the point in doing the right thing now?

I shouldn't continue with our relationship, but he's like a drug I can't quit. I can't say no to him. I'm hooked.

# CHAPTER 23

## *Jenny*
## *February 2008*

I watch Charlie through my bedroom window as she cuts across the lawn. I'm putting myself back together quickly before she wonders why I look like a hot mess. I shooed him out with barely enough time to spare. I don't want to explain him to my family just yet. Eventually I will, if it turns into more, but right now I don't see the point. We are having fun, that's all.

I hear the front door squeak shut as he sneaks out toward the alley. I had him park down the street, so no one questions my "new friend."

Tuesday night is Thai food and movie night. It's been Charlie's and my routine since I moved into my sister's guest house. I like my little house-cum-office setup. It's perfect for me.

We got the awful news that my parents were in a deadly accident when I was in college. I lived with them over summers and breaks, and when we had to sell my parents' house to pay off their debts, I had nowhere to go for breaks. Charlie, my sister

Joan, and her husband Frank welcomed me with open arms and let me stay in their newly renovated guest house. It was perfect. We could all be together and heal as a family. Charlie and I were always close, but now we were even closer. After grad school I decided to make this residence permanent and floated the idea to Joan and Frank about having my practice here too. Frank was resistant at first, but he's a pushover and I finally wore him down. I've been here ever since. I love having them close, except when I'm keeping secrets, I have to be more careful.

"Hey, Jenny," Charlie shouts from the front of my house.

"Be right there, sweetie." I holler back from my bedroom. I quickly pull my hair back in a high ponytail.

Charlie's already eating when I get out to the living room. My sweet, Charlie. I love her to death, but she's a mess. Her hair doesn't look like she combed it today and her oversized hoodie isn't flattering her cute little figure whatsoever. Joan and I try with her, but Charlie is clueless and doesn't respond to our suggestions. She has so much potential. I worry about her so much. Her head is always in her books, which is good, but I want her to experience life. Also, she's never even been on a date and she'll be eighteen in a couple of months.

Charlie smiles as she catches me looking at her. "I got extra spring rolls this time. Ya know, to avoid the spring-roll disaster we had last time—that last one had been mine. You'd had all yours already," Charlie says with a mouth full of food.

"Close your mouth when you speak. And that last spring roll had been mine. I can't help it that you can't count," I playfully joke back.

We both laugh and selfishly reach for our share of the appetizers.

"So, how was your day?" I ask Charlie.

"Eh, uneventful, yours?"

I push around the food on my plate and say, "It was a full day of appointments. I'm beat. I hope I can make it through a whole movie tonight," I lie. Today was actually easy but I'm exhausted from my little playtime with him. I don't dare tell my seventeen-year-old niece that, though.

"Rough life being an adult," Charlie says with a hardy laugh.

"Hey, you're right around the corner, missy. You're almost a college girl now. Are you getting excited for OSU?" I ask her.

"I'm so excited. I'm ready to move on, but I will miss you, and I will miss our Tuesday takeout night. Think you can make the drive to see me each Tuesday?" Charlie says.

"I wish—I'm going to miss you like crazy, kid. It won't be the same without you here. Your parents are going to drive me nuts. I love my sister and Frank, but you've been a nice little buffer," I say jokingly.

"You know I'll be back all the time," Charlie responds.

"You'll get to college, make new friends, get a boyfriend, and you won't have time for your aunt anymore."

"I'll always have time for you. Hey, you going to eat that last spring roll?" Charlie says, and she reaches across the table to my plate.

I smack her hand down playfully. "Not so fast, hands off, this one is all mine." I shove the spring roll into my mouth before she can try again.

"Hey, want to go shopping on Friday? Maybe we could go get our hair cut and a mani-pedi? Fun girls' night out?" I ask, but I already know her response.

"Fun for you. No, thank you. I think I'm just going to stay in and read some of my new books I got yesterday at the bookstore on my way home from school. Plus, I have to finish a book for my English class. Looks like my weekend's already planned out. Sorry, no time to watch you shop," she responds.

"Charlie, when are you ever going to let me take you shopping? I've been trying since you were five and you've always refused. You are one stubborn little girl. One of these days I'm going to get you to change your mind. I guarantee you're going to call me from college and beg me to take you shopping. You just wait and see."

"Can we just watch our movie?" Charlie presses.

"Sure, which do you wanna watch tonight?"

"*10 Things I Hate About You*," she says.

"I swear we just watched that one. Are you sure you don't want to watch *Clueless* instead?"

"We just watched that one too. How about *Mean Girls*?" We both giggle.

"*Mean Girls* it is then," I say.

I get the movie cued up and we spend the night gabbing. I'm going to miss this when she's away.

# CHAPTER 24

### *Charlie*
### *February 2008*

I stare past the two medium coffees that sit on the table in front of me, and I watch the door impatiently. I took the liberty to order for both of us today. Liam's been running late more frequently, and I get more time with him if I grab both coffees and wait for him at our table.

I haven't told him the truth yet.

I'm scared I will lose him the second I do.

Every day I wait for the perfect time but so far, the perfect time hasn't come. I wish for him to ask me on a proper date outside Coffee Loon. Then maybe once he falls hard for me, then I can tell him. Once I turn eighteen, will it even matter to him?

I enjoy and look forward to our lunch dates, but I need more from him.

I'm falling in love with Liam.

Of that I am certain.

I've never felt like this before. I am not sure how to act around him. Is he my boyfriend?

Maybe today, I will ask him what I am to him, but I'm nervous. I need him. I'm addicted to him, and I don't want to scare him away.

My heart leaps as he walks through the parking lot and then through the doorway into the café. With each step he takes, my heart beats faster. His devilish grin has the same effect on me that it did the first time we met. Luckily, I'm sitting, or I may fall weak in the knees and topple over.

"Hey, sorry I'm late. I stayed after class today to work in the darkroom. I had some film I wanted to develop from my snowshoeing excursion last weekend," Liam says as he scatters his photos all over the table for me to view.

"Wow, Liam, these are really good. You're really talented," I gush as I study each photo carefully.

I particularly like the photos of his friends snowshoeing along the river. The sparkling rapids glisten with hints of frost and the reflection of the blue-sky dancing off the water. Absolutely breathtaking.

"Tomorrow, me and my buddy Eric are going to snowshoe up Tumalo Mountain with our snowboards strapped to our packs so we can board back down. I'm going to bring my camera so I can catch some action shots of Eric."

"That sounds really cool," I respond.

"So, I won't be able to meet you tomorrow. I just wanted to stop in and tell you, but I've got to get back to school now. Thanks for the coffee, I'll catch you next week."

And just like that, Liam is gone. My heart drops to the pit of my stomach, giving me an uneasy feeling. He never invites me. He barely gave me five minutes today. Am I losing him? I desperately want to be a more significant part of his adventurous life.

I'm in love with Liam.

***

Back at home, I can't get him out of my head. Liam was short with me today and I try not to read too much into it, but I can't help but feel neglected by him.

Then there's my little secret. I don't think I've lied to Jenny, but I haven't told her the truth either. It's starting to eat at me. I feel guilty, but I know what she will say. She wouldn't approve of our relationship. I've never kept a secret from Jenny. My parents sure, but not her.

I have to focus, and if I don't clear my mind and get my schoolwork done, I'm never going to get out of high school.

Time to concentrate, Charlie.

I've barely opened my book when my mom hollers down the hallway toward me. "Charlie, phone is for you. It's Zoey."

I pick up the phone in the living room. "Hey, Zoey."

"Hey, Charlie, how's it going?" Zoey asks, her voice not sounding like her normal, peppy self.

"I'm good. Things are going fine." Although I'm lying. My tummy is in knots.

I haven't told my friends about Liam yet because I'm not sure what to tell them.

"I feel like we haven't hung out in a while. Want to go get pizza with Mike and me in a little bit?" Zoey asks.

"No, sorry I have to finish reading *The Great Gatsby* for my English class," I respond.

"What's been going on with you lately? Where have you been at lunch? Are you going to the coffee shop? You can't survive on coffee alone," Zoey says accusingly.

"Nothing is going on with me. I've just been busy, and I get a scone from time to time. It's all good. Don't worry about me. Let's go to a movie next weekend."

"Sure, a movie sounds good," Zoey says, but I can tell she wants to keep pressing me for answers.

I cut her off before she can continue. "See ya at school tomorrow. I will meet you at lunch."

Since Liam isn't going to meet me tomorrow, lunch is a promise I know I can keep.

"OK, Charlie, see ya tomorrow," Zoey says, defeated.

Why am I acting like this? I don't know who I am anymore. I changed when he walked into my life.

OK, time to get my schoolwork done. I grab my favorite purple crochet blanket that my grandma made for me before she passed. I cozy up in our bay window on the long, fluffy cushion. Finally, time to find out what happens to Gatsby and Daisy.

An hour passes, and tears flow down my cheeks as I finish the last pages. I can't control my emotions and I can't explain why I feel so much for this book. It's such a tragic story of one man's incapacity to wake up from his illusions and finally accept what is truly real. Sad, twisted story, it really is.

I wipe my eyes with the blanket, and as I'm doing so, something catches my attention.

Jenny is in the backyard. She looks exceptionally pretty today. I mean, she's always beautiful, but something is different today. I've never seen her dress like that for work. She flaunts across the lawn in a low-cut red blouse. Her tiny little frame is put perfectly together in tight black pants and red boots that climb up her skinny long legs. Everything about her outfit is out of place for a winter workday. I watch as she practically skips back inside. Her steps are light and airy as she makes her way to the door that enters into her bedroom. The daylight's almost gone, and her blinds are drawn, but her silhouette appears behind the closed blinds. I'm shocked when a second silhouette enters the room. They move closer together and embrace in a what appears to be a romantic hug. I watch as their lips move closer until they are fully blended into one figure.

Look away, Charlie. You shouldn't be watching. But I'm glued to the silhouette. I can't pull my eyes off it. Who could be at her house? Jenny never mentioned a new guy in her life. I feel a little betrayed that she didn't share this with me. We tell each other everything. Well, almost anything. Suddenly, I don't feel so guilty now. I guess we both have our little secrets.

# CHAPTER 25

## Charlie
## February 2008

A flash of heat rushes over my entire body, and I can't breathe. I'm trapped. I open my mouth again, and the words scratch along my throat, but nothing comes out. Help! Help me.

I'm lying on my back, paralyzed. I want to turn my body, but it refuses to move. The only movement is my chest wheezing up and down. The repetitions are faster now. Sweat pools in the niche above my clavicle, and I desperately want to wipe it away. More hot droplets run across the nape of my neck. My breathing is more labored with each attempt, and my throat wants to close as my breath darts away from me, out of my control.

My hair is wet against my head; I'm burning up. I open my mouth again and the words score my throat. "Someone, please help me." I feel the words, but no sound follows—it's as if I can see them floating out of my mouth and evaporating like water vapor on a cold day. But no cooling relief as I draw in what little breath I can; the words burn my throat. Tears pour out of my eyes as I lay there, wholly helpless, screaming with no noise. My esophagus feels torn, and all I can taste is blood in my mouth. I can't swallow, but merely push all the air in and out of my lungs, faster and faster. The rise and fall of my chest, the taste of blood in my mouth, words that make no sound. Darkness surrounds me. My lungs still snatching at every breath, clamoring for oxygen.

Both sides of my face are soaked with tears, and mucus is streaming from my nose. I want to raise my hand and wipe my face, but my body ignores my request. My chest and stomach are in sync with each other in movement, going up and down. I swear I can hear my parents yelling my name and yelling out for Jenny.

# CHAPTER 26

### Jenny
### February 2008

I fly out of bed and throw open the window. I swear I hear my sister yelling.

"Jenny, Jenny. Wake up, Jenny! We need help!" It is my sister shouting. Joan needs me. Her voice is scared. I immediately know something is very wrong.

I'm coming, Joan.

I dash out, run through the yard, and I hear Joan calling for me again. "Jenny, help, it's Charlie. Jenny, where are you? Help!" my sister screams louder. Her voice is all panic.

I leap up the stairs, taking them three at a time. I bolt into Charlie's room, where I see my sister pacing and still shouting for me. "Jenny, hurry."

"I'm here, Joan. What's going on?" I say, ready to assess the situation.

"I don't know what's wrong with Charlie." Her hand is shaking as she points to Frank on the bed with my niece. He looks like he's trying to wrestle her awake.

I crawl into Charlie's bed and gently nudge Frank away. He gives me an understanding look and moves to the end of the bed. Joan watches me as she continues to pace the room.

Charlie has mucus running down her face and tears pouring from her eyes.

I study Charlie quickly and carefully. Sleep paralysis, perhaps.

"Charlie, sweetie, it's Jenny. Can you hear me?" Nothing.

I stroke her hair to calm her down. I see the terror in her eyes, but I don't want to startle her and make it worse. I'm cautious with my movement. "Charlie," I whisper her name again.

"Sweet, sweet Charlie Bear, It's Jenny. Sweetie, I need you to wake up." I rub her arms and feel that she's burning up and sweating. Her bedsheets are soaked.

Charlie blinks. She's coming around.

I feel relieved, but her breath is darting out faster than before. She seems more alert, but now she's almost panting, trying to control her breath. She's having a full-blown panic attack. "Charlie, I need you to focus on me." I guide her to sit up in bed. I tightly hug her with one arm while Joan places a tissue in my other hand. I wipe her nose and eyes while caressing her cheeks.

I keep my voice low and calm. "Charlie, you got this darling, I'm here in your bedroom with you. Let's concentrate on your breathing. I know this is scary, but you're OK, nothing to fear. Let's take a deep breath in. Try to hold it. Deep breath out.

"Charlie, I'm going to have you try to count your breath. One, two, three, four . . ."

Her breathing slows down the longer I count with her.

"Charlie, I need you to say my name."

"Je-Je-Jenny," she slowly sputters out.

"OK, I want you to point at your dad."

She slowly lifts her hand and points to Frank.

"OK good. You're doing great." I hold her until she can control her breath and then Joan and Frank crawl onto the bed to embrace and comfort her. I move over to the papasan chair across the room to give them space. We all stay until Charlie has calmed down and is safely asleep again.

We quietly sneak downstairs. Joan and Frank are scared and want answers. "Jenny, what was that?" they both ask me.

I'm the professional, but I'm also scared for my niece.

Joan tries to keep herself busy as she scurries around the kitchen looking for the tea kettle. This is how she reacts when she's worried or nervous. She doesn't know how to sit still.

I try to gain my composure for them and use my professional voice. "I know that it was scary to see Charlie like that just now, but I think she may have had some sort of night terrors or sleep paralysis and what you witnessed at the end was definitely a panic attack."

Joan starts crying. "What caused it?"

"Stress or lack of sleep, although there's nothing that I've witnessed from her recently that might have triggered it," I say sadly.

I let my mind wander while they process what I've just said. Charlie has not experienced a tragic event, death, or anything like that, which can sometimes be associated with panic attacks. I haven't seen any signs of anxiety. The only life-changing event is the pending move to college, and she seems excited about that, if anything. I truly can't pinpoint the cause down to anything specific, and I feel like a horrible aunt, friend, and psychologist right now.

Maybe if I hadn't spent so much time with him, I could've seen this coming.

Joan is still rummaging through the cabinets, and Frank gets up to help Joan find the kettle. He fills it with water and paces the room with his wife. "We haven't seen her much lately. Maybe we missed something. I've been so busy at the office and well, Joan was busy at the floral shop with Valentine's Day just ending. No one's really been home for her," Frank says.

"Oh my sweet baby girl," Joan moans.

My beautiful sister. I hate seeing her distraught like this.

"Well, Jenny, I want you to treat her. It has to be you. I don't feel comfortable with anyone but you helping her. She knows you and trusts you," Frank says.

"Oh, Frank, I don't think I can. I don't feel right treating my own niece. I didn't notice anything going on in her life before. What makes you think I can figure it out now?" I spout back in frustration.

"I don't mean professionally sitting her down and talking it out. I mean more like pull it out of her, get her to talk. Watch Charlie. Keep an eye on her. We know something is going on with her, so we want to be aware. You're smart; you will find a good way to evaluate Charlie without actually telling her what you're doing. I don't want to scare her."

I don't understand why he is being so weird about this. It's normal for people to seek therapy for something as simple as a panic attack.

I sit back and cross my arms. "I don't think that's a good idea."

"Please, Jenny. Think about Mom," Joan pleads.

"Fine. I will do what I can."

# CHAPTER 27

### Charlie
### February 2008

My eyes are glued shut and I have to try hard to pry them open. Gross. I feel yucky. I rub my hand along my neck and push away my hair that's stuck to the skin. Visions of my nightmare slowly come back to me. I was trapped and I couldn't breathe. I remember I had no control, and everything was spinning out of my reach. Nothing made sense. I remember Mom, Dad, and Jenny were in my nightmare. Chills flush my body. Gosh, everything about that nightmare feels real right now in the light of day. Bits and pieces flutter back into my memory. It was horrible, but it was just a nightmare. Right?

I slowly make my way out of bed and shove my feet into my slippers. I'm sluggish and tired and barely have the energy to lift my feet and walk. I shuffle my way into the bathroom. My reflection in the mirror appalls me.

I look like shit.

I feel like hell.

I'm fucking ugly.

My dishwater-blonde hair is blah, straggly, and lifeless. My eyebrows are like caterpillars, my nose is slightly crooked, and my lips are too thin. I'm so ugly. I'm not pretty like Jenny or even my mom. I frown at myself in the mirror. No wonder Liam hasn't asked me on a date yet. He's embarrassed by me. Who could ever love me? I am a fool for thinking I could get a guy like him. I am so stupid.

# CHAPTER 28

### Jenny
### March 2008

Dark, ominous clouds roll in fast above me as I make my way across the mall parking lot. A tiny speck of rain kisses my nose. A few more clouds loom over the mountains in view from the parking lot's west end. I can feel the storm is just moments away. I rummage, with one hand, through my black satchel for my car keys as I cross the lot. My darn bag is a catch-all for everything. My keys, lip gloss, and other important items always find a way of ending up in the corners and crevices, annoying the crap out of me. Of course, this bag was designed by a man. A woman would never have done this to herself. I imagine the designer sitting up late in his office, laughing as he plots the most beautiful bags but then makes them useless. The thought irritates me. Note to self— never again buy a handbag designed by a man.

Dang, still no darn car keys.

I stop and use my free hand to lift the bottom of bag up and push the contents into my eyesight.

Finally, the keys!

The rain starts to pick up as I'm almost to my car. More droplets hit the top of my head and bounce off my stupid glasses. I really didn't want to wear them today, but my allergies are so bad that I could not get my contacts into my dry, red eyes. *Dang you, juniper trees, I curse you.*

I hope that since I gave in and wore the glasses today, I can be rewarded tonight by being able to wear my contacts. I really don't want to wear my glasses this evening. Although I was once told I looked like a hot teacher when I do wear them, which I'll take as a compliment.

I open my car door and toss my bag in the passenger seat. As the engine roars to life, the sky above opens up, and tiny pieces of hail mixed with rain pounce off my windshield. I go straight to switch on the windshield wipers when something catches my eye. I open the car door; fresh rain blows against my face, leaving little drops on my glasses; blurring my vision. I reach for the white envelope that is tucked under my wiper blades. It's already sopping wet.

Really? A parking ticket.

I don't see what parking law I'm violating. I will deal with this later. I toss the soggy letter next to my purse. It will have to dry up a little before I can even open it anyway, otherwise, it will just rip, and be a lost cause.

My phone buzzes; I see it is a message from him. A smile spreads across my face, making me forget my little annoyances from moments ago.

*Pick you up at 7. Reservations at 7:15. Wear something sexy ;)*

"I did buy myself something sexy," I say out loud. I'm pretty pleased with my new purchase of a racy yellow dress with a deep

V-neck and a high slit up the right leg. I almost bought the safe black dress that I could also wear to work, but then I thought if I can wear it to work, then it's not a date dress. I can't help but feel giddy thinking about tonight. It's the first real date we've been on outside my house. It's a big step for us. We are taking our relationship out of the bedroom and out on the town. He was so cute the last time we were together. He kept going on about this incredible steak house right here in town. He couldn't believe I have lived here almost my entire life and have never been to this apparently iconic restaurant. I swear he went on for five minutes about these darn steaks. He insisted to take me on a date there. I found it cute how excited he got over food. He is a man who knows what he likes, and right now, he seems to really like me, and, of course, steak.

I know I need to keep my focus on Charlie, but right now, I'm not sure what to do to help her. I've been keeping an eye on her along with Frank and Joan, but tonight I'm going to let myself have a little bit of fun. We don't think Charlie remembers the panic attack or anything from that night. Frank won't let us directly ask her what happened. He thinks it's for the best if she doesn't remember. I told Frank he's just making my job harder by not letting me address it head on, but I have to respect his wishes. I promise my attention and focus will be on her first thing tomorrow. I will get to the bottom of her panic attack.

I finally make it home and pull down the alleyway to park my car. I reach for the bag and my purse from the passenger seat. I almost forget about the little white envelope with my supposed ticket. As I reach back for it and it's almost in my hand, I am caught completely off guard. I must have only seen the back of the envelope when I was in the rain at the mall. It is obviously not a ticket because it's addressed *To Jenny*. It is meant for me.

Who left me a little note?

I run inside and carefully open the letter at my kitchen counter. It's wet and hard to peel out of the envelope. I'm careful so I don't tear the entire thing apart. I rip the edge, but the rest comes out nicely. I spread the damp note out on the countertop to read it.

> *To Jenny,*
> *I know what you've been doing, and it's wrong.*

What? Is this a prank? Some kind of messed-up joke?

No one knows anything about us. Do they?

Guilt for my secret briefly touches the surface, but I push it back down.

If it didn't have my name on it, I would assume it was a mistake. Too much of a coincidence for all that to be for the wrong Jenny. Right?

Could it be from one of my clients? Perhaps Marvin, my ten o'clock appointment this morning. I was distracted during our session, thinking about what I would wear tonight. Did he sense that I wasn't giving him my attention? Or perhaps it was my one o'clock, Beverly? Did one of them follow me to the mall? They've both been known to stalk people and do some crazy things for attention. Both seem unlikely though.

I don't recognize the handwriting. It's sloppy and angry-looking, if handwriting can be angry. Either way, the note doesn't have a pleasant feel. Whoever did this unquestionably wrote it in haste, and the rain didn't help the feel of the note. The letters are practically dripping off the page. I feel like they could pour off the page and puddle at my feet.

Oh, crap. I'm going to be late.

I really don't want to be late. I don't have time to deal with this awful letter from an unknown author. I can't let it consume me, but someone thinks they know something.

I put the letter in the top drawer of my desk. I can figure it out later, but not tonight.

I haven't been this happy in a long time and he makes me happy, so I'm not going to let this note ruin my evening.

I shower and put myself together quickly. I'm happy my eyes are better, and I can wear my contacts.

The dress fits as expected, and my hairstyle works perfectly; down with a few curls scattered throughout. My long brown mane is still pretty and luxurious; most women my age started to see their hair thin or have even turned gray already. This girl I went to high school with turned almost 100 percent gray by the time she was thirty. She didn't even bother to try and cover it up. I know I'm too vain for that and would have to color my hair, at the first sight of gray.

The doorbell rings, interrupting my thoughts.

Oh, he is here! I squeal, a little shriek of excitement.

I answer the door. He smiles his beautiful wide grin and hands me a single red rose. I beam and playfully ask, "What is this for?"

"It's the one-month anniversary since we started dating, or whatever you want to call what we've been doing," he replies and winks at me.

"Oh my," I say, startled by his thoughtfulness. "You are too sweet. Thank you for my rose."

He gives me a coy smile, and I set the flower on the counter. He grabs me around the waist and pulls me into him.

"We've got a few minutes," he whispers into my ear. The warmth from his breath makes my body tingle. He kisses the length of my neck softly and then pulls me into my bedroom. He undoes my dress with one hand, and it slinks off my body and onto the floor. For a brief second, I think about my dress getting wrinkled, but he quickly interrupts my thoughts by pulling me back into the moment with a long, passionate kiss. I yearn for more.

I take my time undressing him. Slow and sexy, but I can sense he's ready to play. He likes to be in control in the bedroom. It's been a nice change for me. I'm always the one in control of every aspect of my life. I never get to just let go and let someone else pull the strings. I get a rush from it.

He prefers things a little kinky and I play along. His confidence in the bedroom is a major turn-on.

"Babe, do you trust me?" he says and he pushes me back onto the bed.

I nod and smile. I watch as he walks over to his pants coiled up on the floor. He pulls two long strings of twine from the pocket.

He struts back to my bed, kisses the top of my forehead, and continues until he has kissed every inch of my body down to my toes. I'm shivering with anticipation.

"Give me your hands," he asks.

I hold them out and he takes one wrist at a time and ties them to each bedpost.

I'm lying face up and spread across the bed with my wrists held hostage firmly in place by my bedposts. Helpless.

"It's not handcuffs, but it will work," he says.

"Well, this is new," I say, with a little uncertainty in my voice. But it's not handcuffs, like he said. I can handle a little twine. I try to reassure myself that this is OK. Not being in control gives me an unknown tingle.

I can let this sexy man take the helm for a few minutes. I will take back some power later, but right now, I will give in. I've read *Fifty Shades of Grey*, so I know what to expect from a man like this.

I relax my body, close my eyes and take a deep breath in, feeling like Anastasia did with Christian Grey.

I prepare myself for the Red Room of Pain, but he is soft and gentle. My hands are tied up, but the sex is sweet. Nothing to be afraid of, Jenny.

He is smooth with his thrusts as he continually pushes his way into me. He continues to kiss my neck softly until he finishes.

"See, that wasn't so bad now, was it? I think you kinda enjoyed the little thrill of it all," he asks.

I blush. "It was a little exciting," I admit.

He unties me. We lie together naked for a few minutes before the realization hits us. "We're going to be late," we both spout out in unison.

I wince at the thought of my sex hair. I spent so much time getting ready and now I look like a hot mess, I'm sure.

"Our little sexual detour might cost us our table at the steak house," I say to him in a sexy tone.

"I will choose you over steak any day, baby," he jokes.

# CHAPTER 29

## Charlie
## March 2008

My foot taps impulsively under the table. I'm more irritated than normal with Liam's tardiness. Each time the door swings open and it's not him, I lose hope. Is he really going to leave me hanging? He wouldn't stand me up, would he? I gnaw anxiously on my nails until my fingers are red.

I'm at our usual table with our usual drinks. Everything is set up as it should be.

I run through all the reasons he could be late. Perhaps his loud muffler finally fell off?

Maybe his niece needed a last-minute sitter.

Maybe he is working late in the darkroom again.

Calm down, Charlie, I'm sure he has a good excuse. You're overreacting.

I pull out my laptop to try and take my mind off him for a minute but it's not working. My anxiety accelerates with each passing minute. My shaking legs are now vibrating the table.

The bell rings across the street. I slam my laptop shut and push it into my backpack.

I grab my drink and walk toward the door glancing back. A Medium Americano with Liam's name written in black sharpie sits on top of our lonely table. If he arrives and finds his cup, he will know that I was here, and he missed me.

Tears fill my eyes as I run out of Coffee Loon. This is not how things are supposed to be going.

# CHAPTER 30

## *Jenny*
## *March 2008*

I invited Charlie over for a girls' night so I can check in and gauge how she is doing since her panic attack. I picked up her favorite Hawaiian pizza. I'm still not sure how I'm going to approach this since my brother-in-law doesn't want me to directly ask her about it. I can't help but feel like I'm about to play mind games with my niece.

Charlie walks through the door in her usual oversized hoodie, sweatpants, and tennis shoes. She plops herself down at the table and goes in for a slice of pizza before even acknowledging my presence. I can't help but study her actions. She looks different and something is off with her. This is the first time I'm noticing a change in her behavior. Was she acting like this before, and we honestly didn't notice?

"Hey, Charlie."

"Hi," she responds. No silly or witty banter follows. She sits in silence as she eats her pizza.

I pull up a chair and put a slice on my plate.

"Only a couple of months left of high school. The countdown is on," I say in an upbeat tone.

"Yep."

"I feel like we haven't gossiped in a while. What's going on with everyone at school. I haven't seen Zoey or Mike around lately. What's going on with them?"

"Mike's been busy. I don't even know if I'd call him a friend anymore. I haven't seen him all semester, really. Zoey is starting to annoy me. Always asking me to hang out and I'm busy with school. I don't have time and she gets mad at me for it."

"Well, I'm sure Zoey is just going to miss you and is afraid you will drift apart when you're both away at school. I hope you don't let that happen, Charlie. Zoey is a good friend. One you should keep forever."

"Whatever. It is what it is," Charlie responds harshly and without heart.

"Anything else going on?" I press on.

"Oh my gosh, Jenny. You're being really annoying right now. Can you just drop it? Nothing is going on. Everything is boring. I'm almost done with school and this place."

She's never given me a lick of attitude before. Something is eating at her, but what on earth could it be?

"What movie should we watch tonight?" I ask, changing the subject.

"I think I'm just going to head home. I'm tired. Thanks for the pizza." She grabs another slice and walks out the door while eating it.

I'm left dumbfounded. What the hell was that?

Maybe she is worried about her life changing and potentially not handling the upcoming change well. Or she could be getting bullied again at school. I remember her sixth-grade bully, Sophia—the pretty little girl with brown hair and freckles. It was a hard year for Charlie. She didn't know how to stand up for herself and she let Sophia bully her all year long. Joan tried to talk to Sophia's parents, but they didn't want to know. Luckily Sophia and her family moved to Seattle, and the bully problem solved itself. Charlie never learned how to cope with a tormentor. Charlie can be very sensitive and always wants to please others. She also prefers to go unnoticed by most people. She is lucky to have Zoey and Mike as friends. They are a little nerdy, but they are good friends—or certainly were—and they all understood each other's weird social quirks. Charlie would be content not having any friends at all and just staying at home eating takeout and reading a good book. I've tried hard to build her confidence. I've let her borrow my clothes, which, of course, didn't fit her as they should, but were still an improvement over her usual clothes. I've tried to do her hair to help her learn how to style it. I've lent her my good jewelry for the school dances I drove her to, but I doubt she ever even went inside. She probably had a book in her purse and sat at the coffee shop across the street for all I know. I've tried to get her excited about college by telling her stories from my university life. Things get better once you go to college. No one knows you, so you get to reinvent yourself. Parties are better and the boys are different—you meet people from all over the country. Of course, I mentioned how great the libraries are, to keep her attention.

I worry for my Charlie Bear. I honestly don't know what else could be eating at my little book worm.

# CHAPTER 31

## *Jenny*
### *March 2008*

I'm still giddy each time he calls to set up a date. I wasn't expecting him to call tonight. I had told him I was busy, so I'm shocked when I see his name on my phone. I can't stop thinking about Charlie and her actions earlier tonight, so I answer his call, welcoming the distraction.

"Hey, doll, I know you said you're busy tonight, but I hoped maybe later I can swing by with a bottle of wine, and we can make a night of it?"

"Sure, why not? My plans changed," I reply.

"OK, I'll head your way now. See ya in a bit."

While I wait for him to arrive, I think about the little white envelope sitting in the top drawer of my desk. What does it mean? Is it about him? Perhaps about my little secret or something else entirely? I truly don't understand why someone would have left that on my car. Maybe someday I will have an answer.

\*\*\*

When he arrives with the wine, I pour us each a glass, and we sit on the couch. We always start on the couch, then we eventually make our way to the bedroom. He has been sweet and playful since our twine night. I smile each time I think of that evening being tied up in my bed. He has not brought the twine out again, although I secretly hope he will tonight.

"How was your day?" I ask him

"Pretty uneventful, yours?" He responds.

"Nothing exciting here either," I say. I don't want to complicate my little secret and tell him about my family problems. I'm not ready to mix my two worlds right now.

"Well, it's a good thing we have tonight to look forward to. It sounds like we could both use a little excitement in our day," he says mischievously.

We finish half the bottle of wine while we cuddle, watching TV. He leans in every few minutes and gives me soft, sweet kisses on my forehead. In that moment, I feel like maybe this is something more serious than I originally thought, which changes everything.

"What do you say we take this into the bedroom?" he says, playfully pulling me off the couch.

I give him a sultry grin and allow him to lead me to my bed. He slams the door shut behind us.

His soft touch changes as soon as he starts undressing me. He is swift and boorish with his movements. His gentle, sweet caresses that I have grown accustomed to are not present. No tender kisses all over my body. It doesn't feel right.

"What's the rush?" I ask.

He nuzzles his head roughly into my breasts and ignores my question. I wrap my fingers through his thick brown hair and pull his head up to my face. I kiss him and he kisses me back and bites my lip, a little too hard.

"Ouch, careful, that hurt," I warn him

I start to unbutton his shirt, but he pulls away and finishes undressing himself fast.

"What's with you tonight?" I ask.

"Nothing," he coldly responds.

I reach down to grab my shirt that's coiled up on the floor. "I'm not feeling this anymore. I think you should go."

He stops my hand and tosses the shirt back on the floor.

"Sorry," he says. But I don't sense sincerity in his words.

What is going on with him? I've never, not once, seen him act like this. What has caused his 180-degree turn in his behavior?

"I really think you should go now. I'm not in the mood anymore," I demand.

He forcefully pushes me down onto the bed. I let out a slight shriek of startlement.

"What are you doing?" I demand.

"I'm giving you want you want," he says. He forces himself on top of me. His tall and strong body has me pinned by his weight. He reaches down to his pants next to my bed and pulls something out of his pocket.

Oh my God, does he really think I'm going to let him tie me up with that damn string right now?

I regret my earlier thoughts about the twine.

I wiggle my body below his and thrash my legs around, trying to struggle free. I hear a clank.

Oh shit. Oh shit!

He actually brought fucking handcuffs this time. The cuffs clink together as he pulls my arm up to the bedpost.

"What the fuck is wrong with you tonight? Get off me, you sick fuck." I thrust my body to try and push him off me. He doesn't move. "I'm saying no. No, no, no. Do you hear me? Stop!"

"What, you don't trust me anymore?" he says with an eerie, unrecognizable voice. It seems to be lower. Threatening.

I can feel him getting hard on top of me.

He first locks one wrist to my bedpost and then the other. I'm stuck.

I rock the bed with my whole body trying to free my hands, knowing darn well that this is a ridiculous idea. Stupid girl, you know you're not getting out of this situation now.

"Stop it. Please stop," I plead.

"Hush, Jenny. Relax," he says calmly.

"Why are you doing this? What is wrong with you?"

I can't believe what is happening right now.

"I thought you wanted this, Jenny? I thought you liked our little sex game the other night?"

"What happened to my sweet, sensitive man? Where the fuck did he go?" I cry.

"Oh, Jenny, you knew this was me all along, and I thought you wanted it. You knew the day I walked into your office that you were going to sleep with me. I suspected that you would be easy the second I laid eyes on you. You just needed some sweet attention first. You could have said no to my advances, but you didn't. You kissed me right back, and we fucked on your desk and then on your couch where your patients sit and tell you all their fucked-up problems. Did that turn you on, Jenny? Isn't that fucked up, Jenny? You did that and you wonder what's wrong with me? That's funny."

"You sick asshole," I scream.

His body still has me pinned down and my arms won't free. I'm screwed.

"You were so nice and sweet and thoughtful. Who was that man?" I demand.

"It's been fun toying with you, Jenny. You know you could lose your license by sleeping with a patient. What would your family think? Do you think they would let you stay here if they found out what you've done?"

"I'm going to call the cops!"

"What, and risk losing it all? I know you won't do that."

"Liam—you are messed up."

"Jenny, I don't think you're supposed to say that to a patient." Liam laughs.

My heart is racing. I thought I knew this man. How am I going to get out of this situation?

"Jenny, it's time to just let go and enjoy our little game," Liam says with a devilish laugh.

Liam thrusts inside me. There is nothing I can do to stop him. His eyes are wild with exhilaration. Tears rush from my eyes as I watch him get even more excited as he witnesses my struggles. He abruptly stops and leans forward.

"Do you trust me?" he whispers in my ear.

I don't respond. Is he fucking joking?

He peers into my eyes, and I watch as his eyes turn darker.

He wraps his large, strong hands around my neck and presses down on my windpipe. I can't breathe.

Is this another one of his games? I don't want to play.

"No, no, no," I manage to say.

He smiles. "You like it nasty, you bitch."

A bang outside against my house stops him. I'm able to turn my head to the window.

Is that Charlie? I try to shout at her, if that's really her. I can't tell. He pulls my head back. No, no, I'm lacking oxygen. I can't breathe. Oh, God. Please. I gasp, but his hands are wrapped so tightly around my throat. It's no longer a sex game. This is serious. He wants to really hurt me.

I try to wrap my legs around his body to thrust him off me. Each time I get momentum, I lose my control. I feel my body getting weaker. My legs quiver until going completely limp.

I see nothing but darkness.

# CHAPTER 32

## *Jenny*
## *March 2008*

My throat is sore. I can't swallow. My mouth is dry, and I desperately need water. I wipe the crusted tears out of the corner of my eyes.

Terror surges over every cell in my body as my wrist comes into view. Blueish-purple bruises surround my entire wrist.

Last night. The handcuffs. Liam.

I'm shivering in fear, my body lying naked on my bed. Alone.

He must have let me go. I check my other hand. It's free from the handcuffs as well, with a similar bruise pushing its way to the surface. My eyes dart around the room, searching every corner. He is gone, and so is any evidence he was here last night. No Liam and no handcuffs.

My left hand tenderly rubs the marks of the right hand's bruise, all the while I am wishing all of this to have been just a bad nightmare but knowing darn well it was not. The evidence is on my wrists. It was real.

A rustle comes from the living room. Is he still in my home? He can't be.

I want to scream. I massage my throat, remembering the choking. I doubt I could even get out a shriek. Even if I could, he would be in here before anyone else could help me. I must have blacked out from the lack of oxygen, or as a defense mechanism to stop the abuse. This realization shakes me to my core. I can't have him come back in here. I can't take another round of his torture.

This can't be happening.

I tightly wrap my naked body in my bedsheet and stumble into my bathroom.

Once in the bathroom, I secure the lock behind me and press my ear up against the door. I don't hear anything. I hope it was just my imagination. Why on earth would he stick around?

My body slumps and slides down the door's length, and I blend into the floor, curled up in the fetal position. I tightly swaddle my naked body in the sheet. I am safe in here. I think. I hope.

Fear, sadness, and anger all wash over me at once.

All that time, he was testing his limits to see what he could get away with before he made his final move. How did I not see this coming? I must be a piss poor psychologist if I didn't notice his psychopathic tendencies. He was calculating and manipulating me, and then his cold-hearted demons came out to play last night.

The smell of bacon wafts under my door. Is he making breakfast in my home after what he did last night?

A loud, hard thump pounds against the door.

He is here.

"Jenny, I know you're in there."

"Leave me alone, go away, Liam," I cry.

"Come out. I made us breakfast." He insists.

"Breakfast. You've got to be fucking kidding me. After last

night. After everything you said and did to me. Do you really think I'm going to come out and eat breakfast with you? What is wrong with you?" I scream and my voice breaks.

My throat is tender from my outburst. I rub it again and wince from the pain that is fueling the fiery anger in me.

"I came to you for help, Jenny. Isn't that what you're supposed to do? So, help me."

"No, I'm pretty sure you came to me because you wanted to manipulate me. You told me you had sleeping issues. I wanted to help you through that. You lied to me, Liam."

"I told you everything last night. I have a sex-addiction problem. I need help," he pleads.

"I'm pretty sure you told me you targeted me, and you raped me last night. You're right about one thing, though—you need some serious help, but I can't help you."

"I'm sorry, I get out of hand sometimes, but I don't mean it. Jenny, babe, let me in," he groans as he pounds his fist against the door.

I hear him slide the weight of his body down and the door moves with each breath he takes.

I need to be as far away from him as possible. I know I'm safe in my locked bathroom, but being that close to him repulses me. I slide my body toward the bathtub and prop myself up against it. I stare at the door, ready to address him.

"Are you fucking kidding me, you sick fuck? Get out of my house, or I will call the cops." I spew my words back at him. I reach for my phone to do just that, but I don't have my phone. It must still be in the living room where I left it last night. Stupid woman. Stupid girl. Why are you so dumb?

Tears flow down my face.

"I need to explain myself to you, Jenny. Please come out here."

His voice is shaking now.

"Explain? Explain how you almost killed me! Explain how you are one sick son of a bitch!" I yell back at him. The volume of my words scores my throat, making it burn with every word I scream.

"Please, Jenny, I love you. I would never hurt you. I got carried away," he says between sobs.

"You don't hurt people you love," I say sadly.

"I love you. I love you. I love you," he repeats the words as if it will make a difference.

He's never said "I love you" before, and I know he is using it as a weapon to make me feel something for him. To make me vulnerable again. I know better, and I can't let my guard down. The only thing I could ever feel for him from now on is anger and fear.

"I'm so sorry, and I didn't mean to hurt you. I got carried away," he says again, repeating his words like they are rehearsed.

I take a long, deep breath to prepare myself for my next question. I feel the therapist in me coming out.

"Liam," I say cautiously. "You've done this before, haven't you?"

"No, I don't think so," he says, but doesn't sound sure at all.

I know he doesn't believe what he's just said.

"Liam, I can't help you. I think you get off by hurting women, and you enjoy dominating them. You need professional help, and I'm not that professional. You hurt me. Don't you get that? You intentionally planned to hurt me."

I can't help but think about the other women he's attacked in the past, and the women he could injure in the future. I want to call the cops and tell them about everything and stop him from doing this to others, but then I remember what he said last night about losing my license and what my family would think about me. I can't risk losing everything over one mistake. One fucked-up mistake.

"Liam, if you love me, you will leave right now. I can't look at you. I need time to think." If I didn't say the last part, I knew he wouldn't leave. He needs to feel there is hope. I need him gone, and I'm going to say anything to make sure he vacates my home.

I hear him back away from the door. I wait a few moments, and I hear the front door slam shut.

I lean over and vomit into the tub.

# CHAPTER 33

### Jenny
### March 2008

I still can't believe what happened to me last night. It seems so surreal. I replay every interaction I have ever had with Liam since he walked into my office. I knew what I was doing and that it was wrong. I knew he was younger than me. I saw every red flag to stop myself before it got started, but I couldn't help myself, and now I'm paying for my actions.

I have to run to clear my mind. Running is my release. I run to heal every emotion and right now I have about fifty different emotions flooding my veins. I feel like I'm going to burst if I don't get out of my house.

I throw on my running clothes, toss my hair into a high ponytail, and slip into my purple Nikes.

I get in my car and have every intention of driving to the river trail. I can't control the panic in my body as I drive, and I feel the need to pull the car over. I'm still a mile away from the trail, but I have to get out now. I have to run. I feel trapped like last night and I need to breathe air now. I swerve and pull up by the side of the road. I get out, and as soon as my feet hit the pavement, I can breathe again. I feel my feet diving toward the ground, harder and faster than my normal stride. Each jaunt is harder than the last. Pain stings its way up my leg, but I don't care. I see his face each time I blink, and I want to stop and cry, but I press on. I'm stronger than this. I fucked up, but I won't let this stop me. I can't let this break me.

Once I make it to the river trail, I stop to catch my breath. There are a lot of people out today. The sun is shining, and it's the perfect spring day to get outside. But I feel anxious when I see all the people. I feel like they know what I did. I feel their eyes watching me. I need to run again. I take off in a full sprint and make the entire river trail loop in a personal record time. I've never run so fast before.

I'm exhausted now and regretting my dire need to leave my car earlier. I don't have any more energy to run. I sulk all the way back to my car. I feel the pain of last night setting back in. My wrists burn as the sweat runs over my injuries. My tummy grumbles—I couldn't bear to cook anything in a kitchen where he spent his morning waiting for me. I left his breakfast of bacon and eggs sitting on the countertop. I might have to toss the entire plate in the trash when I get home. The thought of him in my kitchen makes me ill. My mile walk back to my car is feeling more like three miles.

As I approach my car, I notice another one of those little white envelopes tucked under my wiper blade. Are you kidding me? I run over to my car and rip it from the windshield.

*To Jenny, the whore.*

This time I don't wait until I'm home. I open my car door, slide inside, and rip it open, desperate to see what is inside.

I still don't recognize the handwriting. My hands tremble and the paper shakes in my fingertips.

> *To Jenny, the whore,*
> *You slut. I know what you did. You're still doing it. I've seen you.*

I pound my fist into the dashboard.

I don't know how much more of this I can take. I feel like I'm losing my mind.

Is Liam messing with me? It has to be him. He is the only one who would be so cruel. Is he following me? I immediately feel like I'm being watched. I put my car into drive and race home as quickly as possible.

Everything I ever knew about life, about people, about everything is crumbling into the tiniest pieces.

# CHAPTER 34

## *Jenny*
## *April 2008*

The last two weeks have been a struggle for me. I told my patients that I have the flu, and can't shake it—a lie, of course. I had to keep my bruises hidden until they healed. I need time to regroup and put the pieces of my psyche back together. Those tiny little pieces that Liam shattered me into. The shards of those pieces that the mysterious white envelopes left me in. They wounded me and left me fragmented. I'm not sure if I will ever be whole again. I thought I was stronger than this, but I'm struggling. I wish I could talk to my sister, but I'm dying inside from the guilt I have from my lies and secrets. I want to tell my family, but I fear they will judge me. I can't risk losing everything I built here. My home, my practice, and the trust I have from everyone around me. I'm sick to my stomach.

And then there is Charlie. I feel like absolute rubbish about leaving her hanging. Something is clearly eating at her, enough to cause her panic attack. I've been so self-absorbed dealing with my own problems that I've let her issue go to the wayside. At least she has no idea I'm leaving her out to dry, but it still doesn't make it right. I have kept a watchful eye on the house during my downtime. I have barely seen Charlie leave, except for school. She didn't even ask how I was feeling, not once, and that is not like her. I have texted her and all I get back are one-word responses.

I'm failing at everything in life right now.

My phone vibrates. It's a message from Liam. The third one since that horrible night. My body goes numb.

> *Please, can we talk? You said you would help me. You wouldn't lie to me, would you?*

It's the same as the last two. My plan is to keep ignoring him. I feel that it is all I can do. That horrendous night in my bedroom seeps back into my memories. The handcuffs, his eyes, his awful words, the choking. I rub my wrists, which are healed now, and my throat feels better too, but the memory of that night will be with me forever. The psychologist in me wants to dive in and figure out why he did what he did, but the victim he made of me won't let me even touch the surface of his problems.

I turn my phone off and decide to get outside for some fresh air. I've been trapped in my house for two weeks. I didn't want anyone to see me. I bought myself some time away from the family with my made-up flu. No one wanted to get sick, so they kept their distance. Joan left soup on my doorstep on more than one occasion, but for the most part they let me be. But now with my conjectured flu gone, I have to pretend I'm OK, but I'm not OK.

Once outside, I'm about to take a seat at our patio table when I see Joan.

"Hey, good to see you out and about. Some flu you had. I hope you're doing better now," Joan says.

"I'm tired, but I'm doing good," I respond. All lies.

Joan takes a seat next to me. Her eyes are red and puffy. "I know you've been sick, but we need to get back on track with Charlie. She had another panic attack last night. I calmed her down like you did last time."

"Why didn't you call me?" I respond.

"We had it under control. It wasn't as bad as the first one. It only lasted a few moments," Joan says.

"I know I've been ill, but you really should have called me. I should have been there. Especially if you want me to treat her," I lecture my sister. "How has she been lately?"

"Well, here's another thing. Her school called yesterday. She's been missing her history class after her lunch period. They said they left me a couple of messages on our answering machine at home, but Charlie must have deleted them, because we never got the messages."

"What? Charlie would never miss a class. That's not like her," I respond.

Joan shifts in her chair. "I'm really worried. When I asked her about it, she completely ignored me and shut me out. She stomped off to her bedroom and slammed the door. She's been on that darn laptop of hers all the time, and that's it. She hasn't done anything outside the house. We have no idea what she's doing after lunch."

I feel guilt pinging its way down my entire body.

I watch as Joan wipes the tears from her eyes. She continues. "So, I couldn't help myself, and I called her friend Zoey to see if she knew what's been going on with Charlie. I didn't tell her about the panic attacks, of course. That information is only for the family's ears. Zoey said Charlie has been quiet and withdrawn lately. She barely says two words to her at school and they haven't hung out in weeks. That was all she knew. She seemed worried about Charlie too."

I'm in absolute shock. This is not like my niece at all. "Do you think that maybe Charlie is finally being a normal teenager and rebelling like you did when you were her age?" I ask my sister.

"You were nine when I was Charlie's age. How do you remember what I was like?" Joan questions. "And, no, I know my daughter, and this is not stupid rebellious stuff."

"I looked up to my big sister. I watched your every move. You had a wild side. Maybe Charlie got a little of that from you." I push back to my sister's response.

"I promise you, it's not like that. It's different," Joan shouts. "I know my daughter, and trust I know her better than you do."

I'm not sure how true her last statement is. I feel like I spend more time with Charlie than she does.

"Well then, Joan, we are losing time. She is going to be leaving soon, and we need to figure this out. I think it might be time we look into other professionals for help."

"Jenny, we really need you to help her. It has to be you," Joan demands.

"Why does it have to be me? Help is help." I shout, demanding an answer.

I'm not in the right frame of mind to help Charlie the way she needs to be helped. I want to tell my sister I'm broken right now, but I don't.

"Remember when you told me about that hypnotherapy study clinic you did in grad school? Do you think you could try it on Charlie?" Joan asks.

"Oh, no, Joan, I don't think that's a good idea."

"Please, Jenny. Frank and I discussed it, and we don't know what else to do. You have to try for us."

"I will think about it," I say, feeling overly defeated by my older sister.

# CHAPTER 35

### Jenny
### May 2008

I have to get back into my routine. I can't let everything going on keep me down. I've been disconnected and out of sorts. This has gone on for far too long and it is even more clear now that it's not going to stop. The text messages I received this morning still have me shaken.

> *Jenny. Are you ignoring me? I wouldn't do that if I were you. Answer me now!*

I want to block his number, but I don't want to be caught off guard. I have to stay alert and know what's coming next. If I block him, then I would be blind to his actions.

I've been leaving the house less and less to avoid any sort of encounter from Liam or the author of my notes. I have zero food left in my house, so the grocery store is first on my to-do list. I have to go on with my life or he wins.

As I walk through the store, I feel everyone's eyes on me. I know it's all in my head, but I feel like I have the words, guilty, victim, and fool written in marker on my face.

I'm having a hard time looking people in the eye. I keep my head down and work my way through my grocery list. My phone vibrates, another text message from Liam.

*Don't forget the bacon, sweetie.*

He's watching me. He knows that I am at the grocery store. My eyes dart around. My head is spinning.

Liam is following me.

I am in public, so he can't hurt me here. Right?

My heart descends down into my stomach. He is stepping up his game. Taunting me. Waiting for me to react. That is exactly what he wants. He wants to see me squirm. I cannot react. I am not calm, but I have to pretend to be. I finish grabbing the last few items on my grocery list and make my way to the cash register.

Another text from him.

*Did you get the red wine I like?*

Seriously. This has to stop. He is like a cat playing with its prey before it goes in for the kill.

I unload my cart. The cashier asks me a question, probably about the weather or if I found everything OK. I honestly don't know. I just smile and nod and continue about my business.

The bag boy loads my bags into the cart, and I wheel it to my car. My eyes dash quickly through the parking lot. His old beat-up car is parked at the end of the lot. He speeds away when he sees me. His car is quiet now. That sneaky son-of-a-bitch got his muffler fixed. He knew I would be listening for his loud noise-polluting piece of trash. I cannot help but put my middle finger in the air as he pulls out of the parking lot and speeds away.

Once I am safe in my car and driving home, I let my emotions play out. I scream. I cry. I even laugh. The kind of laugh that makes you question your sanity.

Why is he tormenting me? Did he not get enough that night? He's harassing, threatening, and stalking me. I know I need to go to the police, but the thought makes me recoil. That would mean telling my story, and I don't think I'm ready to relive that just yet. I am also not prepared for the repercussions of what will happen when I tell the police I slept with my patient while I was treating him. I am not ready for my family to hear how unethical I have been, and I'm most definitely not ready to say I was held hostage on my bed while I was taunted, handcuffed, raped, and then choked until I blacked out. I'm just not ready for all that. I don't want Charlie to hear any of it, especially right now. I could not bear if this makes her condition worse. I've already had to be sneaky to gather what I have so far to help her. She has no idea. This could make things worse. So much worse.

I fucked up.

I really fucked up.

I turn on the music as loud as I can tolerate it. I have to tune out the world.

When I pull up to my house and park my car, I can sense something is not right. My front door is slightly open.

Maybe it's just Frank. He said he would fix the loose floorboard in my living room, but he would have given me a heads-up. He respects my privacy. Charlie has been known to let herself into my house before, but given her current circumstances, I highly doubt it is her. She has been keeping her distance from me, and everyone, for that matter.

I slowly step out of my car and locate my mace and take it from my purse. I hold it tightly in one hand. My phone is secure in my back pocket for easy reach and my car keys in the other, pointing straight forward as a potential weapon.

I cautiously nudge the door open with the mace out in front of me.

I shakily let out, "Hello, who's there? Joan? Frank? Charlie?" No response.

I hear someone shuffling their feet across the hardwood floor in my bedroom. I raise my hand higher, showing I am not afraid to use the mace.

Liam steps out from my bedroom. He has his hands in the air like he is surrendering to the police.

"Whoa, Jenny. It's just me. You don't need that mace now, do you?" He smiles as he lowers his hands.

I keep my arm straight forward, ready to spray. The sight of him repulses me. I want to run, but I know that is what he wants from me. I have to stay strong.

"What are you doing here? You have to leave. Get out now!" I shout.

He steps forward, leaving my bedroom and entering into my living area.

I shout again. "You have to go, please get the hell out of my house."

"Jenny, I wanted to see you," he says with sincerity in his voice. Spoken like a true psychopath.

I now understand how easily people can be manipulated by their abusers. I'm not going to play that game. My eyes are open now and I can't be fooled again.

"I brought you a gift." He gestures over to my kitchen counter.

A single red rose and a monkey stuffed animal with a heart in its arms sit on my counter.

I feel the bile rising in my throat. I swallow it. I will not show him any weakness.

"Why are you following me? Why are you doing this to me?" I say.

He smiles an eerie smile.

"Liam, I really need you to get out."

Liam takes a wary step forward and then another.

"Stop or I'll scream."

"Jenny, if you were going to do something about me, you would've done it by now. Tsk, tsk, tsk, Dr. Jenny, whatcha going do about it now?"

Before I know it. He lunges forward and grabs me around the waist. I drop my mace and keys. He has a hold of my body with one strong arm and then he covers my mouth with the other. Memories of him choking me cause me to panic. I thrust my body harder.

No, no, this can't be happening.

I try to wiggle my body from his embrace, but he is just too strong. I feel like he has gotten even more muscular since the last time.

Liam whispers into my ear, "I told you not to ignore me, Jenny."

I stomp down on his foot, but it does no good. He's like a beast.

The main house's back door slams shut. "Someone is coming," I try to say, but his hand is too tight across my mouth. I bite him with my front teeth, but they just graze the epidermis.

"What am I going to do about you, Jenny?" Liam hisses in my ear. His breath is hot against my skin.

I hear the crunch of footsteps in the gravel path outside. Someone will be in here in just a matter of seconds. They will see me in danger, and they will run and call the cops.

My bedroom door to the backyard squeaks open. I try to shout again. A little noise comes out. Liam hears the door this time as it shuts.

He drops my entire body in one swift motion. I fall to the floor. One hard thump and I am on the ground. Liam runs out the front door, avoiding being seen or caught.

"Hello! Help!" I shout.

My door slams again.

"Hello? Is anyone there? Charlie?" I yell into the empty abyss of my home.

I get up and run to the backdoor. No one is there. I head back through my house and open the front door. I glance in both directions and Liam appears to be long gone, but when I turn around to go back inside, I see what is taped to the front door. Another little white envelope.

Fuck you, Liam. Haven't you done enough damage to my mental state and now you have to play this sick game with me too? Still, my hands quiver as I reach for the note. This little twist to his game is getting immature and pedestrian. I don't understand it.

I rip the note down that is taped to the door. *To Jenny, the bitchface.* How fucking clever is that.

*To Jenny, the bitchface.*
*Now I'm just pissed. How could you do this? You fucking slut. You might be pretty, but you're fucking dumb.*

Dumb is right. I should have thrown the stupid note in the trash. I'm over this childish game.

But what if it's not Liam, and it's . . . no . . . I shake my thought from out of my head before I even let myself entertain it.

# CHAPTER 36

## *Jenny*
## *May 2008*

I can't sleep. The sun is creeping into my room and I'm not sure I even got a full hour's rest. I don't want to think about last night, but I have to. My mind has been spinning like a hamster on a wheel. Round and round, and round and round. How did he get into my home? Is he still watching me? Who snuck into my house yesterday when he was here? Could it have been Charlie? Did she see us together? I heard the back door. I swear I did. I'm pretty sure I did. It couldn't have been in my head. The noise scared him away. Then there are the notes. I can't figure out why. My suspicions and thoughts are overwhelming me, and everything that is spinning through my mind has me sick to my stomach.

I have let Liam torment me for two months and let Charlie slip through my cracks. I'm worse off now than if I would have just gone to the police the day after the handcuff night. I was afraid, but now I'm even more scared. I don't know how far Liam is willing to go. I have to do something now before things get even worse and more out of hand.

And on top of all that, today is Charlie's graduation.

I failed her. I failed myself. I failed Frank and Joan. I even in some sick twisted way failed Liam.

I really need to refer Charlie to another professional.

I'm scared of what I don't understand. I am scared of Liam. I'm scared of what the truth will do to everyone around me.

Any minute now my alarm is going to go off, so I may as well give up on the notion of actually getting any sleep. I need to get a run in before graduation; I have to get a little bit of clarity before I can go on with today. I take a long, warm shower while I continue to figure out my plan. I feel someone is always watching me now. I feel like I'm dirty even though I'm in the shower.

***

I need to stay calm if I'm going to get through the day. Don't forget to breathe, Jenny. I tell myself over and over the entire jog down to the river trail. In . . . out . . . in . . .out. I can do this.

The morning dew kisses my face, and a chill runs down my back. I don't know if the chill is from the wet breeze or the complicated fact that everything is going to change after today. Charlie, Liam, it's all going to be addressed tonight. While I was in the shower, I confirmed I must go to the police. Liam isn't going to stop. This is going to change everything for me, my career, my home, and my family, but I have to. I will tell Frank and Joan we need to have someone else treat Charlie. I just can't do it anymore. I will wait until after graduation. I want Charlie to be able to have her moment and enjoy graduation before everything blows up.

As I approach my running trail, I glance around to get my bearings. Everything seems normal. I don't see Liam or his car anywhere. I should be OK, although I still can't help but feel like

I'm being watched. I start off at a slow pace as I turn onto my trail. The sun is coming up in the east, showcasing the beautiful snowcapped mountains. It's such a beautiful morning. I need to enjoy this moment. Breathe in . . . out . . .

The ground is soaked with the fresh morning dew. I know I need to be careful and watch my step; I can't afford to slip and fall today.

I'm startled when I hear branches rustling up ahead of me. I'm cautious as I approach. Please don't be Liam.

Oh, thank goodness, it's just a sweet little deer. Not Liam. I'm relieved. I take off faster and further into the trees. Cars and city noises are fading behind with each step I take. With each press of my foot to the ground, I feel like I'm finding myself again, and it encourages me to go faster and pick up my pace. The faster I run, the safer I feel. Well, that is until I see a runner on the other side of the river.

The person is in a dark hoodie, with the hood pulled over their head. There is a chill in the air, so maybe it's to keep warm and it's nothing to fear, but the person seems to be mirroring my pace. Normal, happy, unfucked-up Jenny would usually welcome the friendly competition and wave to the fellow runner. But scared, frightened Jenny feels fear. I pick up my pace and the runner continues to mirror me. I slow down and they do too. I have to be imagining this. I run up an incline and stop at the top to catch my breath. I see the runner across the river stopping down below as well. The runner waves at me. But it doesn't feel friendly. The wave is slow and unnerving. Is this all in my head? Then the person takes off in the direction they came from. Oh, thank God. A massive sense of relief rushes over me. I'm being paranoid and almost let that person ruin my run and my favorite place along the river. I need to start taking back control. I can't be afraid anymore. I won't be a victim. To Liam, or even to my imagination.

I weave in and out of the trees, feeling light as air, only stopping one more time to catch my breath before reaching the bridge to cross the river. I walk to the middle of the bridge. I stop to take in the beauty and a few deep breaths to center myself again.

"I wish I could stay here forever," I say out loud.

I feel the bridge swaying under me.

"Oh, pretty, pretty, Jenny, you *can* stay here forever." A voice whispers.

I scream.

# CHAPTER 37

### Charlie
### May 2008

It's Saturday morning and graduation day. The weather is beautiful, and the sun is shining. I can't help but smile. In just a few short hours, I will be free. Free from the confines of high-school life and at midnight tonight, I will be eighteen. Officially an adult. I can do what I want. It will be the start of my new life and I have a good feeling about things to come. Now, if I could just fast forward to August, then I would be really happy. Everyone has been driving me nuts lately. My parents are hovering, and even Jenny has been acting strange. Something is off with her, and she's been absent recently. I've been feeling anxious too—probably all the coffee. I haven't seen Liam in a month. He was quiet the last time I saw him. He didn't have much to say. We practically sat in silence. Tomorrow I will tell him we can be together.

\*\*\*

I'm standing in the doorway at home. I went out this morning, and I know my mom is going to yell at me for being late. I'm watching my dad run around the house. He doesn't even notice me in the doorway.

"Hey, I'm home," I finally say.

My dad smiles at me and continues running around the house from room to room. "Where's the camera?" he shouts to my mom. "I can't find it."

"It's in the hallway closet," Mom yells from upstairs.

I watch as Dad runs over to the closet. "Ah, here it is. Found it."

"Don't forget the tissues."

It's almost humorous watching them buzz around. They care more about today than I do.

My mom runs down the stairs and sees me standing in the doorway. She has a displeased look on her face.

"Charlie! Where were you all morning? I've been calling you." My mother touts in a high-pitched tone. My mom looks exceptionally nice today. Her light brown hair is pinned back neatly, and she's wearing a long floral dress that accentuates her curves.

I look down at my phone. "I didn't hear it ring. It must be on silent."

My mom frowns. "So, what's your excuse? Where were you?"

"I told you I was having breakfast with Zoey and Mike this morning."

My mom looks shocked by my response. She knows I'm lying. I didn't tell her, but I thought maybe she wouldn't remember and just let it go.

"Dear, I would have remembered that today. I don't think you told me. I wouldn't have agreed to that on such a big day. But it doesn't matter now. Come on. You need to go upstairs and get ready. You look like something the cat dragged in." She says and shoos me up the stairs.

My mom follows me into my bedroom. "Can you please do something with that hair of yours? It's a mess. I can curl it for you if you'd like? Or maybe Jenny can come over and help you get ready if you don't want your mother doing it for you."

"No, Mom, I will be fine. I don't need anyone's help to get ready. I'm going to be wearing a cap and gown. No one is even going to notice that I didn't curl my hair," I respond in a sarcastic voice.

"What do you think happens after the ceremony? People usually take off the cap and gown. I laid out one of Jenny's dresses for you to wear under the gown. It might be a little tight, but you didn't have anything suitable in your closet, and you wouldn't let us take you shopping," Mom says not letting me get my way.

"OK, Mom, I will curl my hair and wear the stupid dress," I respond, hoping that will be the end of it.

"Please hurry, Charlie—we don't want to be late," she says and walks out of my room.

I love my mom, I do, but sometimes she can be a little bossy. She and Jenny always want me to wear my hair a certain way or want me to dress how they think a high-schooler should dress. Mom is just more blunt about it. Jenny at least tries to be subtle.

I get ready quickly to avoid being yelled at. My mom failed to lay shoes out for me, so I slip into my black flip flops.

"I'm ready to go," I shout as I make my way down the hall. My mom smiles and seems pleased with my promptness and the fact I followed her instructions for once. I try to cover my feet, so she doesn't see my choice in footwear. She seems too busy to notice. Looks like I get to wear my choice in shoes. I can't help but smile.

"Frank! Are you ready? We need to leave. Frank! We can't be late," my mom hollers.

"Sorry, Joan, I just wanted to make sure I had the extra camera battery. We can't miss our Charlie Bear's big moment!" Dad says as he tousles the top of my head. My mom cringes as it messes up my curls. So, of course, I love it.

"Frank, have you heard from Jenny today?" My mom asks.

"No, I haven't seen or heard from her," he replies.

Mom looks at me questioningly, and I shake my head.

"Where the hell is she? What is going on with that woman lately?" My mom, who loves being in control, says, clearly annoyed. When people don't do what they say they will do, or be where they say they will be, it irritates her.

I can't help but wonder where Jenny is though. It's not like her to be late. She should be here. First, my tardiness, and now Jenny's. Mom isn't pleased.

"I'm going to run over to the guest house real quick and see what's going on," she says.

My mom always refers to Jenny's place as the "guest house," even though Jenny has lived there full-time since she graduated from college. I don't think Jenny has ever minded, but it always bothers me for her. It's her house, not a guest house anymore. Get it right, Mom.

My dad and I wait in silence. Dad tends to get sentimental on days like today. He cried like a baby at my junior-high graduation. I didn't want to say anything that would send him off in tears.

When Mom appears, she has a worried look on her face. "She's not home. I wonder where she could be? I will just text her to meet us there, I guess. We can't wait any longer or Charlie Bear will miss her big day," she says as she corrals us to the door.

"She is probably just out buying me a last-minute gift or flowers," I tell her.

She smiles. "You're probably right."

***

When we arrive at the school, Mike, Zoey, and their families are waiting outside.

"Hey there, Faye family," Mike's dad says excitedly as we walk up to them. "We haven't seen you guys in ages."

Mike smiles at me, and Zoey gives me a hug.

"I miss you," she whispers in my ear. "You're still coming to my party, right?" she asks softly.

"Yah, I will be there." I grin.

"Hey guys, I need a picture of the three musketeers all grown up," my dad says as he forces Mike, Zoey, and I all together. "Smile!" We smile to please my dad, but none of us really wants to be together right now. We've already started to drift apart, but I don't think any of our parents have got the memo.

"Hey, Bob, can you take a family photo of us?" Dad asks Zoey's father as he pushes his camera into his hands and then feels the need to instruct him how to use a camera like the man's never operated one before.

"Sure, hey, let's get Jenny in your photo. Where is she?" Bob says as he gazes around us, searching for my aunt.

"She's on her way," my mom responds with uncertainty in her voice.

I can't help but feel uneasy about Jenny missing our family photo.

We smile for Bob and impatiently wait for him to snap the perfect shot.

We all make our way inside. One big group. Our teachers instruct the graduates to leave our parents and make our way into the auditorium.

In my assigned seat, I gaze around the auditorium, trying to locate my parents. Of course, I spot them in the front row, waving excitedly at me when they catch me staring at them. My mom's cardigan is placed on the chair next to hers, reserving it for Jenny.

I shift in my seat, feeling more anxious now. Jenny would never miss this moment. Where is she?

During the entire ceremony, I keep checking over my shoulder to see if she arrived, but she never does.

Once the ceremony is over, and our caps have been tossed into the air in celebration, I meet back up with my parents. I'm sad. I'm worried. I'm anxious.

As I make my way over to my parents, I see my mom has a distressed look on her face, which makes me feel even more uneasy. Once she sees me, her expression quickly changes to a smile. She doesn't want me to worry, but I'm more anxious now than ever.

"We are so proud of you, Charlie," Mom says, giving me a huge hug. My dad joins in on the embrace.

"Jenny isn't here, is she?" I ask, already knowing the answer.

"No, sweetie, I'm afraid she missed it. I'm sure she has a good explanation," my mom says.

"Should we get a few more photos?" Dad suggests.

"No, I only want one of me and Jenny." I pout.

Zoey is making her way back over to my family and me. "Charlie, I will see you at my party at six, right? If you want, you can come early and help me finish setting up. You want to ride with us?" Zoey says excitedly.

My mind is so distracted thinking about where Jenny could be that I snap. "God, Zoey! I know it's your party, but today isn't just about you. I will be there when I get there!"

I can't believe the words that come out of my mouth. Zoey stares back at me like she is going to cry. She is only trying to be nice and connect with me, and I've snapped at her. I feel bad, but I can't help it. I need to know why Jenny missed my graduation.

"Charlie, I've tried with you. I don't know what's going on with you lately, but don't bother coming if you're going to act like this. You're being a bitch," Zoey shouts.

"Girls, that's no way to talk to each other. We need to get going, but Charlie will be there at six," Mom promises.

"Mom!" I shout, irritated with her for sticking her nose in.

All three of us walk back to the car in silence. I think my mom is embarrassed by my outburst. I feel bad for how I reacted. I know I shouldn't have spoken to Zoey like that.

The fifteen-minute drive to our house feels like an eternity. I can't stop imagining the worst.

As we round the corner by our house, we see flashing lights. "Did someone get pulled over?" I ask Dad. He doesn't respond, but I see fear in his eyes in the reflection in the rearview mirror.

The closer we get, the brighter the lights. "Dad, what is going on? Mom?" I shout.

"It's OK, sweetie." My mom says as she reaches back and rubs my knee.

Four cop cars are directly in front of our house. My heart sinks to the pit of my stomach.

Dad pulls the car into the driveway.

All three of us are deadly silent now, all thinking the worst and hoping we are wrong.

Mom opens the car door before Dad puts the car into park. I watch her run the length of our front yard.

My dad and I are right behind her, but before we can reach my mom, we watch her fall to the ground and as she lets out a bloodcurdling scream.

I drop to the grass and mimic my mother's loud cry. I know. My dad knows.

Aunt Jenny is dead.

# CHAPTER 38

### *Charlie*
### *May 2008*

The officers help us inside. They have us sit down in our spacious living room. Everything is still a blur. I have a gut feeling about what's happened, but the words haven't been said to me yet. I only know because of my mother's reaction that my aunt is dead. What else could it be? Tears flood down my face, and I feel like I've been punched in the gut.

A man in a nice suit enters the room.

"My name is Detective Morgan. I have some difficult news. It's my understanding that you're Jenny Morrison's sister," the man says as he looks kindly toward my mom.

She nods, and more tears flood down her face. The detective continues. "I'm sorry to tell you this, but Jenny's body was found this morning by a group of joggers down by the river. She was pronounced dead on the scene when our officers arrived. Her body is being transferred to the medical examiner for an autopsy. I'm sad to tell you this, but we suspect foul play. I'm sorry for your loss, but rest assured we have all our best men and women working on this."

My dad stutters out," I, I, don't understand. What do you mean, her body was found?"

Mom hasn't stopped crying and a pile of tissues is stacking up in front of her. She looks like she is going to go into shock.

"Her body was found in the water, under the footbridge on the river trail. We think she was out for a jog, and someone attacked her. The cause of death is still undetermined, but my team is working on it right now. We will have answers soon. I know this is extremely difficult to hear."

"This doesn't make any sense. How do you know it is Jenny?" Dad breaks out in tears.

He has to speak for the family because my mom can't get a word out and I'm not sure what to do.

"She had her ID and phone on her. The phone was pretty much useless because of the water damage, but her ID was intact," the detective tells us. He looks genuinely remorseful for the information he has had to deliver.

"Since we suspect foul play, and we don't know if it is a singled-out attack, or random. We have to ask you some difficult questions, I'm afraid," Detective Morgan says.

"If this wasn't time sensitive, we could do this later, but we don't know if our community is at risk. So, I have to ask you now, OK?"

My dad gives him a sorrowful look of understanding and nods, giving the detective his cue to continue.

"When was the last time each of you saw her?" Detective Morgan asks.

I space out while my parents answer and when it is my turn, I try to recall the last time we spoke, and I honestly don't recall anything for days. "I think it was last week, but I can't remember for sure," I say as my voice cracks over every word.

I can't remember the last thing we said to each other. I can't remember the last dinner we had together. The realization that we won't be able to make any more memories hits me like a ton of bricks. I feel the wind being knocked from my lungs, and I can't catch my breath. Jenny is really gone. This is real. I am not dreaming.

"Do you know of anyone who would want to harm Jenny?" the detective asks.

I can barely understand my mom through her mournful weeping. "No, she was absolutely wonderful to every person she ever encountered. She was the sweetest soul you could imagine. No, I can't think of a single person who would want to harm my sister."

"Did Jenny have a boyfriend?"

"No, she didn't," my dad responds for us.

My stomach turns. I feel a sense of disorientation, as if I'm watching a movie. This can't be real.

The detective asks us more questions, but all I can do is focus on the growing pile of tissues in front of my mom.

"Can you tell me what Jenny does for work?"

"She is— was a psychologist. Her office and home are down there in our guest house." Dad points down the yard to Jenny's home.

"Did she ever mentioned being afraid of one of her patients?"

"No, never," my dad responds and my mom shakes her head from side to side.

"We are going to need to take a look around her house. Can you get us the keys?"

Dad goes into the kitchen and comes back with a key ring and hands it to an officer. The officer leaves the room. I suspect they are going to rummage through her entire life. This really can't be happening. This can't be real.

My thoughts are jumbled. I'm confused. I'm broken. I don't understand the words I'm about to say, but my mouth blurts them out before I can even think and pull them back.

"It was Liam! Liam Sutter. He did it!"

# PART THREE

# CHAPTER 39

*Charlie*
*August 2012*

My phone is clutched tightly in my hand when I awake. It hurts to release my fingers from the death grip around the case. Quinn's not in her bed and I have no missed messages from her. The room is exactly how I left it last night. Quinn hasn't been here. Where is she? Where is Asher? What happened last night? I'm desperate for answers.

I feel clearer today. Thankfully, the boozy feeling of yesterday has worn off. I send a flood of texts to Quinn again. Surely, she would be awake now? That's if she's OK.

*Where are you?*

*I'm worried!*

*Are you OK?*

*Where are you?*

*Please answer!*

*QUINN, please call me now!*

No response.

My phone is nearly dead—I forgot to charge it when I came in last night. I will need a full battery. I can't chance missing a message from Quinn. I need to search for her. I will retrace my steps from last night. Maybe something will jog my memory.

While I wait for my phone to charge, I take a long, hot shower. Once again letting the water scold my skin. I need to feel something, so I know I'm not dreaming. I wince as the water rushes over my body. Definitely not a dream.

I can see pinkish bruises forming just above my left knee. I have scratches along the inside of my forearm. From the pebbles, perhaps? I honestly don't know.

After my shower, I examine my head in the mirror. Nothing about it has changed since last night. It is still just a small little cut. I do my best to part my hair so it covers my tiny little gash.

I need another change of clothes, so I change into Quinn's clothes, pulling something from her open suitcase out on the floor. I pull out a white tank top with a large anchor on the front and a pair of jean shorts. I slip on my Converse sneakers. This will do.

The realization that I need to check out of the hotel before eleven today hits me. Oh, crap. Maybe I should book the room for another night. If I can't find Quinn before checkout, I will need a place to stay. I want her to know she can come find me here.

I ring the front desk. "Hi, I'm calling from Room 802, and I was wondering if I could extend my stay another night?"

"Let me take a look. Um, ma'am, it appears you are already booked until the end of the week. You don't need to check out today, unless you want to check out early?"

"Oh, no. That's perfect. Thank you," I respond with composure. I wait for the lady to hang up and I slam the phone down, befuddled. What? Why did she book the hotel for an entire week? Did she plan to have me stay with her? None of this makes any sense. She lives in this dang town. What on earth does she need a week-long reservation for?

I find the address for the restaurant that I snuck into last night. I'm going to work my way backward until I find something. Anything. Any hint to Quinn's whereabouts. Plus, I need to make sure that I didn't leave any traces behind in the restroom. I was highly inebriated and could've made a mistake. I don't know what to think about all that blood that was on me, and until Quinn shows up, I have to be careful with my actions. I would never hurt her, though. Why would I?

*** 

As it turns out, the restaurant is not a far walk from the hotel. I didn't remember much from my cab drive home last night. I had too much on my mind.

I think it will be best if I walk. I will have time to think and process, and hopefully remember more details, if I'm on foot.

Everything looks different in the light of the day when I approach the restaurant. I check the time and it looks as if they have just opened. My hope is to go in undetected so I can check out the restroom and get in and out quickly. I rush inside, walk past the hostess stand, toward the bathroom when the hostess cuts me off.

"A table for one?" she asks.

"I would like to just use the restroom, if that's OK?" I reply.

"The restrooms are for customers only. We have a lot of homeless people cleaning themselves up in our downtown restrooms, so we have a strict policy of customers only."

Do I look homeless to this lady? I am wearing Quinn's clothes. Quinn would be so offended.

I have to give in. Dammit. "Fine," I respond. "I will take a table for one."

I'm thankful for the lazy hostess from last night. If Miss Guard Dog had been on duty last night, things could have gone very differently, and for the worse, I suspect. I'm grateful that no one saw me and my blood-soaked face. People would have asked questions that I had, and still have, no answers to.

The hostess leads me over to a small table near the window that is strategically placed for loners. "Your waiter will be Bill," she says.

I frown at her and she walks away.

The restaurant has an Irish pub feel to it. I didn't notice that last night. Rugby jerseys line the wall along with Jameson, Guinness, and shamrock signs. I imagine this isn't what a real Irish pub looks like.

Bill is prompt and approaches my table before I can sneak away to the bathroom. "Hi, I'm Bill. Can I get you something to drink?"

Vodka on the rocks, please, is what I want to say but I respond with, "Just an iced tea will be fine."

He turns away to grab my drink. I decide it's an excellent time to use the restroom. I pass by the hostess station with the rude girl glaring at me the entire way to the bathroom. Once inside, I search for anything I could have left last night or anything that I missed cleaning up. I'm sure they've cleaned since I was here last,

but I had to check. I just had to know. I don't see any evidence of
my time here last night.

The thought of dashing outside and ditching out on my tea
crosses my mind, but the hostess doesn't shake her glare as I walk
past her again. I wouldn't put it past her to chase me down, tackle
me to the ground, and drag me back inside and force me to order
food. She would probably sit there and watch me eat it too.

Oh, screw it.

I take off out the door and run down the block, and I don't
dare look back.

That was kind of a rush.

I navigate my way back to the dark alley where I woke up last
night. I truly have no idea why I would have come here. Maybe
someone brought me here and I fought them. That would explain
the excess blood on my body. I don't see any blood here where
I laid last night. Nothing seems out of the ordinary. I search the
entire block for signs of Quinn.

"Quinn!" I shout out.

I text her again.

> *I'm really starting to freak out, Quinn. Where are you? If I did
> something and you don't want to talk to me, that's fine, but please let
> me know you're OK.*

I track my way back to where the festival was yesterday, and it's
a longer walk that I could have managed in my state. Something
happened between point A and point B. But what? I walk to the
spot where I last remember seeing Quinn. Nothing.

What about Asher? He said he parked in an event-parking
garage. I bet it is the garage down the street. It is nearby, and they
could get away with charging thirty dollars for nearby parking.

\*\*\*

A silver Mercedes-Benz is parked in the third stall on the first level of the parking lot. If this is his car, I'm lucky to have spotted it right away in this massive garage. Maybe this is a sign of some good luck to come. I peak in through the passenger-side window and see Quinn's champagne-pink cardigan sitting on the seat just as she left it yesterday. This is Asher's car. I can't help but feel emotional when I see her cardigan. Champagne pink is Quinn's signature color, and she always looks pretty when she wears it.

The high of finding his car wears off as I can't help but think, now what?

And where is Asher?

# CHAPTER 40

*Charlie*
*August 2012*

Back at the hotel, I pace the room. Asher did not come back for his car. If he caught a cab last night, he would surely be back by now. Right? Quinn has been missing for almost a day. I haven't heard a word from her. Not one peep to let me know she is safe. Surely, if she saw my worrisome texts and numerous calls, she would contact me? Is this like the night from college that I don't remember? She disappeared from my life three months ago—how is this different?

This time it involves blood and possibly Asher. That's how it's different.

I clearly blacked out both times though, and I don't recall a thing from either night. I also don't remember how I got to Liam's house just a couple of days ago, either. I feel like I'm losing my mind. What is going on with me? I'm losing my mind and I'm losing time.

I text Quinn again. She has to answer this one. If she is messing with me or mad at me, this one will make her come out of hiding.

*I'm going to the police. If you're messing with me. Give it up now.*
*I'm so worried about you.*
*Please respond!*

Nothing.

The thought of actually going through with going to the police has me shaking. Just thinking about the cops gives me chills, and bits and pieces of a clouded memory flood back into my consciousness.

Jenny. Foul Play. Liam Sutter.

The fucking police. They were so kind until I said Liam's name. Everything changed the second I said Liam did it. Everything changed with my parents, the investigation. My entire life.

I close my eyes and count to five. One, two, three, four, five. I take a deep breath and let that memory drift back into the darkness where it needs to stay.

Where are you, Quinn Sullivan?

\*\*\*

I park my car at the police station, but I am having a hard time opening the door. I don't know what I'm doing here. I'm not a 100 percent sure Quinn is really missing, and if I had anything to do with it, then I'm a stupid, dumb girl for being here. I look down at the scratches on my arm. I look guilty. I have nothing to cover them up. My fingers grip the latch, but the movement I need to physically open the door isn't there.

What exactly am I going to report? My friend comes in and out of my life from time to time. She gets mad at me and never tells me what I've done wrong. She could be on a sex binge with her boyfriend. I know where his car is, but I can't find him. I sound untrustworthy and I know what cops do with untrustworthy people.

# CHAPTER 41

*Charlie*
*May 2008*

Detective Morgan's eyes dart directly to me. "Who is Liam Sutter?"

My parents stare at me through tear-filled eyes. "Who?" My mom asks with concern and fear in her quivering voice.

Detective Morgan looks at my parents and then back at me. "Can you tell me who this Liam person is, and why you would think he killed your aunt?"

I stare at them blankly.

I'm so confused.

Did I say that out loud?

Everyone is looking at me for answers, and I don't know what to say.

I don't know why I would have said that. Why would I think my Liam would have anything to do with Jenny's death? Liam is my little secret. Why would I say that?

I'm utterly and completely mixed-up, and nothing makes sense inside my head.

What did I just do?

# CHAPTER 42

## Charlie
## August 2012

A hard knock on my window interrupts my internal debate. A lady with dark brown hair and thick-framed glasses is standing outside my car, looking down into my vehicle.

"Ma'am, ma'am? Are you OK? My name is Officer Francis Dorman. Can you roll your window down, please?" The officer motions for me to roll down the window.

I acknowledge her action, and Officer Dorman asks me again. "Ma'am, are you OK? I've been sitting in my patrol car over there—"she points to her dirty white patrol car backed into a parking space "— and I've been watching you for about ten minutes. You looked passed out and maybe extremely bothered by something. Have you been drinking, ma'am, or have you taken any drugs?"

"Oh, my gosh, Officer. No, I'm sorry. I'm here to report a friend missing. I have not seen or heard from her in twenty-four hours."

Well, crap. The words came out. I guess I have to go through with it now.

"I've just been in a panic all morning because I can't find my friend. I guess I didn't realize that I've been sitting here that long," I respond.

Officer Dorman is staring at me. I'm sure she's judging my credibility.

"I'm sorry, officer, to worry you. I would gladly take a test. I haven't been drinking or anything."

"No, I don't think that will be necessary. How about I walk you inside and help you get your friend reported missing?" she responds and pushes her glasses up that had slid down her nose.

"Thank you, Officer," I reply, and give her a kind smile. See I'm not drunk or on drugs.

She assists me inside the police station and leads me down a narrow, well-lit hallway, and says, "I will have you wait here. I'm going to talk to someone and will be right back. What is your name, my dear?"

"Charlie Faye," I say softly.

I am waiting for about fifteen minutes when Officer Dorman comes back with a man in a blue suit. He isn't wearing the same uniform as Officer Dorman, so I assume he must be the detective.

He doesn't remind me of Detective Morgan whatsoever.

"Miss Faye, Charlie Faye?" he says, staring me up and down.

I nod. "Yes."

"I'm Detective James Hubbard. My colleague here tells me your friend is missing. What is the name of the missing person? How long has the person been missing?"

"Um," is all I can say. I'm starting to sweat. I'm feeling nervous. This is a bad idea. "Um, since yesterday," I stutter. "Her name is Quinn Sullivan."

Detective Hubbard moves closer toward me. I'm getting more nervous. Is this all part of his schtick? Can he see me sweating? Does he sense the fear rushing through my body?

"About what time did you last see her?"

I slowly proceed, thinking of each word as it leaves my mouth. "I think it was late afternoon."

"And where was that at exactly?" he asks.

"We were at the beer festival downtown at Waterfront Park," I respond. I can only guess what he's thinking when I say *beer festival*. Drunk girls, no doubt.

I study him as he jots down some notes. He's a stout man, but bulky from his muscles. The lighting is reflecting off the top of his shiny bald head. He has a stern face and lacks kindness in his features.

"Was anyone else with you?" he says, breathing heavily. His nose squeals each time he takes a breath in.

"Yes, her boyfriend, Asher. I just met him yesterday. I don't know how to contact him, and I don't have his last name."

I'm feeling more of my nerves setting in. I don't know how much more I want to tell him. I feel the scratches on my forearms burning. I look guilty. I feel guilty. I quickly turn my forearms toward the floor, wishing I had worn long sleeves or had something to cover them up.

Detective Hubbard ignores my sudden movement.

"Can you tell me the last thing that happened before she went missing?" he asks.

I speak carefully, choosing what I want to divulge. I want my friend found safe, but I don't want to implicate myself in case I had anything to do with this. Which, of course, I didn't.

"We were at the festival, and I saw her fighting with Asher. I tried to follow her but . . ." I trail off. I don't want to tell him I was drunk and blacked out. " . . . She was too quick, and I have been trying to get ahold of her since, and she won't respond to my calls or messages." My voice has hints of panic in it. I'm sure the detective is picking up on that detail now too.

"Hmm, I see," the detective says as he scratches his shiny, bald head.

"Miss Faye, do you think it's possible that your friend met back up with Asher, and they went somewhere to 'make up'?" he says, using finger quotes when saying makeup, like I don't know what he was implying.

"Detective, I understand what you're saying, but it doesn't feel right. I feel like she would have called me by now to let me know she is OK. I have been calling and texting her nonstop since last night. She was also my ride home. I don't know why she would have purposely left me alone if she was going somewhere to 'make up' with Asher." I copy his air quotes to make him feel silly for using them.

He gives me a coy smile. He realizes I'm poking fun at him.

"I think she would have contacted me by now. I told her that I was going to the police in my last message, so if she was just having sex with her boyfriend, I think she would have responded and told me not to report her missing," I say, a hint of attitude in my voice.

"Asher's car is still parked where he left it yesterday too, if that helps with anything. It's a silver Mercedes-Benz parked in the large parking garage by Waterfront Park. It's in the third stall on the first level. So, they didn't leave in his car to go make up."

"Well, miss, I will have you leave me all her info. Full name, phone number, address, places where she might go, her parents' information, and anything you think will be helpful." His voice is disinterested and robotic. Gosh, he doesn't believe me. He doesn't think she is indeed missing. I knew this would happen. He's convinced himself that she is just with her boyfriend and I'm overreacting.

I get all of Quinn's personal info from my phone. Luckily, I have her home address saved with her contact information.

While I'm waiting for Detective Hubbard to process the information and the facts I gave him, he has Officer Dorman stay with me like I am a criminal that was going to escape.

"It's going to be OK. I'm sure your friend will turn up," Officer Dorman says, trying to give me some hope.

I don't even acknowledge her; I'm too busy watching Hubbard. He is on the phone, and he looks displeased. He hangs up the telephone and walks back over to Officer Dorman and me.

He takes a deep huff in and says, "I tried the phone number you gave me for Quinn. Miss Faye, are you sure this is the right phone number? I called it, and it says it's no longer in use."

How could that possibly be? Did his fat fingers dial the number correctly?

"I'm positive that is the correct number for her," I say, almost shouting. I'm beginning to feel personally attacked by this man.

Hubbard doesn't try to comfort me; he says things just as he thinks them. "Maybe your friend doesn't want to be found. Sometimes that ends up being the case. We will look into it and get back to you."

My heart sinks. What if he is right? What if Quinn doesn't want me to track her down? But why?

I leave him my contact information in case he has a breakthrough, which I highly doubt he will.

I leave the police station regretting my decision to come here. Once I get back to my car, I call Quinn's phone.

*"The phone number you are trying to reach is no longer in service. If you*

*feel you've received this message in error, please try your call again."*
No! That can't be right. That just can't be right.

# CHAPTER 43

### Charlie
### August 2012

It has been hours since I left the police station. I drove around aimlessly before coming back to the hotel. I honestly don't know how to process anything right now. How is Quinn's phone number not in use anymore? I just don't understand. How could that be? It was working just fine yesterday, and now the service has been turned off?

I pick up my phone to try her number for the millionth time, hoping for a different result, when my screen lights up and a Portland area code flashes across it. My heart drops. Could it be Quinn calling? It's the first time my phone has rung in days. I quickly answer with hope in my voice.

"Hello!"

"Hello, Charlie Faye?" I recognize the voice before he even says it.

"Yes, this is Charlie."

"This is Detective James Hubbard from the Portland Metro

PD. I want to speak to you about your friend, Quinn Sullivan. I checked the information you gave me today, and we don't have any record of a Quinn Naomi Sullivan residing at 939 Bridgeport Way. No Peter or Jane Sullivan either. At this point I'm led to believe, that your friend either isn't who she says she is and has been lying to you, or you are pulling our leg. Miss Faye, we do not tolerate that here, and it is a crime to utilize the PD under false pretenses. This is not a joke. Real people go missing all the time. Miss Faye, what do you have to say about all of this?"

I find myself grinding my teeth as he speaks to me. I unclench my jaw to reply to him. "First off, Detective, my friend is missing, and I know her name is Quinn Naomi Sullivan. We have been friends for almost four years. She wouldn't lie to me. I still haven't heard from her, and what if she is in danger? I don't know why or what to believe about what you said, but I know my friend needs me, and I need to help her. Can you understand that, Detective?"

A deep breath and sigh comes from the other end of the phone line, and Detective Hubbard, in an elevated, deep voice, now almost lecturing me, responds. "Well, miss, I don't know what we can do until we have more information on your friend. To me, it sounds like she doesn't want to be found, and if that is the case, then she isn't who she really says she is, and that's not a good friend in my book. Things can be black and white, and things can be gray. Let us know if you find out anything else. We will keep the case open for the time being. Have a good day, Miss Faye."

I throw my phone against the wall in anger.

How could the police not help me? What is wrong with this detective?

The police never seem to believe me.

I retrieve my phone. Luckily, it didn't break. I tried to call Quinn one more time, hoping things will be different.

*"The phone number you are trying to reach is no longer in service. If you feel you've received this message in error, please try your call again."* I end the call and slump down in front of the bed and cry.

I've known Quinn for four years. Sure, she is self-centered from time to time, but she cares about me. She wouldn't have lied to me for our entire friendship. Her parents, she told me all about them. Peter and Jane Sullivan from Portland. They lived here in Portland their entire lives. Her dad works at a factory and her mom is a secretary. Quinn talked to her parents every Monday morning before her classes. I wish I had a phone number for them. I need to find them so they can help me.

I do have their address, though. Maybe Detective Hubbard didn't really check out the information I gave him.

Time to do some investigating on my own.

# CHAPTER 44

### Charlie
### August 2012

I sit in my car at 939 Bridgeport Way. This is where Quinn supposedly grew up and her family still resides.

Where are you, Quinn? Give me some sort of clue.

I glance up and down the street, secretly hoping for any sign of her. So far nothing out of the ordinary.

I'm not sure what to do now that I'm actually here. I have never met her parents, but I do not have a problem confronting them about their daughter. Maybe they can give me a little insight as to why she is the way she is. She would not shut off her phone without giving her parents an updated number, would she?

939 Bridgeport Way is an old brick house with a swing set in the front yard. A large cherry tree houses a beat-up tire swing. I don't recall Quinn ever telling me what her home looked like. So, I'm not sure what to think. She doesn't have any siblings, so I do not know why they would still have a swing set and tire swing. A for-sale sign sits in the corner of the lot. Quinn didn't tell me

her parents are moving. Come to think of it, she said we couldn't meet here because of home renovations. I see no signs of a home renovation either.

I have more questions now than I came here with. I slam my car door shut and walk swiftly across the lawn and up to the front porch. My heart is beating fast. I'm rehearsing lines in my head. Mr. and Mrs. Sullivan, do you know where Quinn is? I can't find your daughter. I think your daughter is lying to me. I think your daughter is in trouble. I think . . . I think . . . but I don't know a thing.

I rap my knuckles hard against the wooden door. I impatiently knock a second time. I wait a minute and as I'm in mid-pivot to turn around and leave, a little boy opens the door. He blurts out, "My mom is on the potty, hold on a second!" He slams the door in my face. Quinn said she didn't have siblings, especially ones this young. This explains the swing set. An only child, she told me; just like me. We bonded over that. I feel defeated. This can't be Quinn's house. I attempt to walk away again, and the door opens a second time. "Hold on, girl, my mom is coming." Again, he slams the door.

I hear a lady beyond the large wood door yelling to the kid, "Who is at the door, honey?"

The door opens for a third time and a slender lady with no makeup appears this time. "Hello, can I help you?" she says politely and then not one, but two little boys peak out from behind their mother. Identical twins. Cute little kids but I'm not in the mood for their games. I need answers. This woman is way too young to be Quinn's mom, Jane.

At this point I realize that Quinn doesn't currently reside here, but has she ever lived here? Did she lie to me about this? I let the words fly out of my mouth. "I saw your house was for sale. I'm very interested and wondered if I could have a look at the place."

The lady with the two boys responds. "Yes, of course. I'm Karen, and these are my boys, Ryan and David. I apologize for the mess. It's hard to keep up with these two sometimes. I swear the house was clean before I took a shower, and then I get out of the shower, and it looks like this." With a wave of the hand, she leads me into the house.

"I'm Marie, by the way," I say. Another lie. They just keep coming out of my mouth. I am shocked at the ease of my fabrications.

I continue, "My husband and I are looking for a home in the Portland area. I'm in town for business, and we plan to move here in three months. I was driving through this neighborhood, thinking how nice it would be to live here, and then I saw your sign and thought, how perfect. I must stop."

I tuck my left hand into my pocket to avoid Karen questioning the lack of a diamond on my ring finger.

Karen smiles at me. "Oh, that is wonderful. We just love this house, but we've outgrown it. These two keep growing, and so does their toy collection."

Wow, Karen, you're way too trusting. Do you ever watch the news? I could be some deranged psycho that you just let into your home.

"Let me show you around the place," Karen says as she guides me through the first level. "Let me know if you have any questions."

"How long have you lived here?" I ask.

"Oh, let's see. I think it's been about seven years now," Karen says as she's counting the years on her fingers.

Seven years! I think I have my answer. Quinn lied. I want to turn around and leave, but Karen's phone rings. She gives me an apologetic look and says, "Please excuse me."

I smile and the boys continue to stare at me. I can't run out on this sweet, trusting lady. What kind of person would scare someone like that? I may be a liar now, but I'm not that cruel.

One of the boys yanks on my hand. "Hey, are you going to buy our house?"

"Uh, maybe," I say. I'm already in my lie. No turning back. May as well play along.

"You can live in my brother's room. I have a monster that lives in my closet—you shouldn't live in my room," he says.

The second boy asks while tugging on my other hand, "Do you have a dog?"

"Um, yes, his name is Shaggy," I respond.

"That's a funny name for a dog," he says, giggling.

I need my two shadows to leave me alone.

"I'm going to have a huge room at my new house. My mommy told me so," my second shadow tells me.

I have to get out of here. Karen, where are you?

It's clear that Quinn doesn't or has ever lived in this house. This is a dead end. I'm not going to find Quinn here.

"Sorry about that," Karen says as she enters the room.

I smile and say, "Your boys were sweet and showed me the rest of the rooms. Thank you for your time. I think I've seen what I need to. I will talk to my husband. Thanks again. Enjoy your day."

I'm back in my car and I want to scream. I'm beyond livid.

Why would Quinn need to lie about where she lived? What is the point of this kind of lie?

Is the detective right?

Yet again, I have more questions than I had when I started my day. This morning I needed to find my friend and now I'm left with the plaguing question of who the hell is Quinn Sullivan?

Who is this girl who posed as my best friend for four years? Yes, Quinn has lied to me a few times over the years—and who doesn't?—but they had been little lies. Things normal girls lie and fight about, such as boys. Not this gigantic monster of a lie.

Shortly after Quinn moved in, I heard a guy in her bedroom. When I asked her, who was in there, she told me it was no one and that I was imagining things. Then Nash, the guy from the frat party, appeared from her room. When I confronted her about it, she just laughed and shook it off like it was all a joke. That should have been a red-flag.

This is a different kind of lie, though—a secret life kind of lie.

I've been running all over this town looking for her, and now I'm starting to question if she is even missing. I have zero answers to what happened to her, Asher, and even what the hell happened to me.

I can't take this anymore. I need to go home. I can't be here any longer. I did what I could. Maybe Quinn doesn't want to be found like Hubbard suggested.

I don't feel well. I want to vomit. Yep, my stomach is churning. I can't swallow it down. I quickly open the car door and it all comes out on the pavement.

Screw Quinn! Look what she is doing to me.

I'm going to head back to the hotel, gather my things, and head back to Bend. I have my own life to live, and I can't let Quinn and her lies control me. If I stay here and try to find her—the 'her' that she clearly isn't—then I'm playing her game and letting her win.

I think I might even take her suitcase with me. In case she comes back, she can figure it out, and she can come find me and her belongings.

# CHAPTER 45

### Charlie
### May 2012

"Can you believe it?" Quinn says as she barges into my room and throws my blinds open. I pull my arm over my eyes to avoid being blinded by the sunlight.

"God, woman, what time is it?" I groggily ask.

"It's seven a.m.! Get up! Can you believe today is the day?" she says, pouncing around my room.

I stare blankly at her, still half asleep.

"Our party, dum-dum," Quinn says, giving me a pitiful look.

I watch as she tosses items from my closet. "Nope. This won't do. Can't wear that. No way in hell." A pile of Quinn's rejected clothes piles up outside my closet. "You will have to wear something of mine."

"Quinn, can this wait? The party isn't until this evening. I need more sleep. We just finished finals, and I'm exhausted." I bury my head under the sheet.

"Even more of a reason to get up. We just finished our senior year of college. We need to celebrate now. We can't waste another second sleeping. We only have our apartment for three more weeks, our home for the past four years—doesn't that mean anything to you? Who would have thought that we would have stayed here that long? I'm going to miss the crap out of this place."

"I'm going to miss this place too, but can't we just have a chill night in?" I plead.

Quinn shakes her head at me. "Nope, wheels are already in motion and this party train can't be stopped."

I catch Nash out of the corner of my eye. He is shirtless and making his way down the hall. I hear the bathroom door close. I'm not going to miss Nash walking around like he lives here.

"Come on, get out of bed. I need help getting the last of the party supplies for tonight," Quinn says, pulling at my arm, attempting to drag me out of bed.

"OK, fine. Give me a second to wake up at least," I say, giving in to Quinn.

"We are going to have so much fun tonight! This will be a party we will never forget."

# CHAPTER 46

## *Charlie*
## *August 2012*

I haven't been in here in four years. Four long, hard years without Jenny. I need to be close to her right now. She would know what to do about Quinn. She would have helped me through this. I need my aunt Jenny right now. Jenny, help me.

I feel like she is still here. Everything is exactly how she left it the morning she went for her run. A few things were removed by the police for their investigation, but for the most part, all her belongings are here, like she is here. My parents could not bear to move her things. I think they thought that if they did, then she would really be gone. They pretty much locked the door and pretended the house didn't exist the moment after the police ended their investigation. That is how they coped. I cannot blame them. I ran halfway across the country to deal with it. The pain from missing her stings every inch of my body.

I pull a bottle of vodka from off her shelf. I wipe four years' worth of dust away with the inside of my shirt, Quinn's shirt. I pull a few swigs from the bottle. I used to think vodka tasted like hand sanitizer, but I've grown accustomed to the taste. I just need to numb my pain. The pain of Quinn, Jenny, and all the questions running rampant in my brain. The drive home did a number on me. I let my mind wander and it took me to dark places with even more questions needing answers. I take a few more pulls from the bottle and stumble over to Jenny's couch.

"Jenny, I could use some fucking help here!" I shout to an empty room.

I half expect her to walk through the front door with a pint of Ben and Jerry's Cherry Garcia ice cream. When one of us had a problem, we would talk it out over ice cream. I stumble back into her kitchen. I open her cabinet; her ice cream dishes are sitting on the second shelf, with a few layers of dust resting on the top bowl. I reach down and pull open the drawer below the counter and, as I expected, see our Micky Mouse ice-cream spoons still there. Jenny bought them at a garage sale as a joke, but we ended up using them each time we had our evening indulgence. We would laugh and eat as we found solutions to our problems together. I pick up one of the spoons and grip it tight. This stupid, ugly spoon that now has such sweet memories attached to it. The day we brought them home from that crappy yard sale, I never thought I would be sitting here getting sentimental over them. I take the spoon and my vodka back to the couch and I let my entire weight plop down, and particles of dust puff up from my abrupt movement and make their way into the air. I watch as they float past me in what's left of the daylight that's shining through her living-room window. I lie down and stare up at the ceiling. I feel like one of her patients. Liam once sat on this couch. How did things go so wrong?

I picture Jenny over at her big oak desk, asking her patients questions and taking notes. She always wore these white glasses that made her look smart. Not that she needed them to add to her smarts. She was an intelligent person. The smartest person I knew. She helped so many people and could have helped so many more if she were still here. A tear rolls down my cheek.

My eyes search the room for something to wipe my face with, and I spot of box of tissues, conveniently placed, just as Jenny left them, on the end table for her patients. I pull the box off the table.

The table wobbles. An eerie creak echoes through the empty house.

This creak would have annoyed Jenny. She would not have tolerated this noise each time someone grabbed a tissue from the table. I don't remember ever noticing it before. She preferred everything neat, tidy, and perfect. I know she is gone but I feel I have to fix it for her.

The table and couch sit on top of a beautiful ivory rug. I lift the table up and place it on the hardwood floor behind me. It is sturdy. It must be the floor. I pull the rug back to expose the flooring underneath, and a loose floorboard creaks again. If Jenny had ever noticed this, she would have asked my dad to fix it. He enjoyed repairing things around the house. Maybe Jenny didn't mention it to him because she broke it and didn't want my dad to be mad at her.

Something feels out of place about this board.

I reach back to the couch for my spoon. My swift movement makes me a little dizzy. Too much booze already. I jam Micky's little head under the floorboard. It is surprisingly easy to jimmy up and with only a little damage to the spoon.

I remove the board and set it next to the couch. I'm shocked when I see there is actually something in the floor.

A small, dusty cherrywood box is sitting inside the ground. I pick it up and use Quinn's shirt to dust off the top.

Are my eyes playing tricks on me?

I'm horrified and my heart stops when I see the label on the box.

In Jenny's perfect handwriting.

*Charlie's Sessions*

# CHAPTER 47

### Charlie
### August 2012

*Charlie's Sessions.* The words are there, but the meaning is not. I have no idea how long I've been staring at this box, but the fading daylight gives me some indication. Charlie's sessions. It doesn't make any sense to me. I keep studying the words, hoping for clarity, but clarity does not come. Nothing but confusion and tipsiness here. I shouldn't have drunk the vodka. I desperately want to have a clear head right now, but it's too late. What's done is done, and I have to see the contents of this box.

My hand vibrates in fear as I flip the top open, rattling the contents.

Inside the box are three cassette tapes, the kind Jenny uses for her patients' sessions so she can transcribe her notes later after the patients leave. On the spine of each tape is a number.

One. Two. Three.

Tucked tightly next to the tapes are four little white envelopes. I grab them and lay them on the floor next to me. Each one is addressed to Jenny in extremely sloppy handwriting. I don't recognize the handwriting at all. I carefully open each envelope. Some are more tattered than others.

The first note is water-stained and sticks to the inside. I'm careful as I pull it out.

> *To Jenny,*
> *I know what you've been doing, and it's wrong.*

Who saw Jenny do what? What on earth is this person talking about? It couldn't be my Jenny they are talking about. They must have the wrong person. It couldn't be my Jenny. I repeat over and over.

The second note comes out easier, but I want to shove it back inside when I see the hateful words on the page.

> *To Jenny, the whore,*
> *You slut. I know what you did. You're still doing it. I've seen you.*

Someone was watching Jenny. But who?

The third note twitches in my hand. I'm afraid of the can of worms I'm about to open with the next one.

> *To Jenny, the bitchface,*
> *Now I'm just pissed. How could you do this? You fucking slut. You might be pretty, but you're fucking dumb.*

The words are so harsh. Tears flood my eyes and run down my face. I feel them dripping off my chin. I don't even want to look at the final one. Each note gets more hateful than the last. I don't know if I can handle what's inside of the last one. I wipe my tears and I'm in complete shock when I see the final note.

*To Jenny, the nasty slut whore who ruined my life,*
*The pretty ones deserve what they get. The pretty ones deserve to die.*

Oh, my fucking God. These notes have something to do with Jenny's death.

I rub my eyes to ensure that what I'm seeing is actually real. I can't believe it. How can this be? My lungs inflate with a long, panicky breath. The stagnant air burns my chest. I grab the bottle of vodka and take another drink. I know I said I want to be clear-minded, but I don't think it matters anymore. Everything is fucked up. I stare back down at the notes and cry. Aunt Jenny. Wonderful, sweet, pretty Aunt Jenny.

# CHAPTER 48

### Charlie
### July 2008

*Main Suspect in Psychologist Murder has Been Cleared.*

We heard the news from the cops last night. They were kind enough to pay us a visit and deliver the news in person. When the newspaper hit our door this morning, we already knew what the headline would be. However, seeing it in print made it more real.

> *Liam Sutter, 21, was cleared this morning as the main suspect in the murder of local psychologist Dr. Jenny Morrison, 33, due to a lack of physical evidence.*

> *Sutter had been romantically involved with the suspect before her murder back in May. Morrison's body was found in the Deschutes River under the footbridge by local joggers. When police were made aware Liam Sutter was involved with the victim, he immediately became a person of interest. Later evidence showed that Sutter was a former patient of Morrison's. He admitted to dating Morrison during*

*his treatment, but they kept their relationship a secret because of the nature of their involvement. He was later quoted saying he didn't think anyone knew that they were dating. They both kept a tight lid on their relationship.*

*The deep bruising on Morrison's windpipe suggested old and new damage. Sutter eventually admitted to choking her when they played sex games during their consensual sexual encounters. All evidence concluded that he did choke her, but police were unable to produce any conclusive evidence that he murdered Morrison. The old bruises matched up with his testimony, but the new ones didn't.*

This is absolute garbage.

The article goes on to show the timeline of Liam's involvement with Jenny and his supposed "witch hunt" by the media. They have also interviewed his sister, roommates, co-workers, and anyone else who knew Liam and would only have nothing but good things to say about him. After all the months of trashing him, the paper wants to cover their ass, now having to redeem him and attempting to give him his life back.

Bullshit, bullshit, bullshit. This is not right. Not fair and not accurate.

The people they interviewed shared sob stories about how his life was now ruined, and he's been devastated by the accusations. The family mentioned me a few times and how I ruined his life by giving his name to the police. The article stated that I only met him once, which he lied about.

Liam, you fucking liar!

Now, his friends and family are defending his love for Jenny. The poor guy lost the love of his life and was a suspect in her murder. They justified his secret romance with his once therapist by saying things to make him look like a saint. Their forbidden affair would have gotten Jenny in trouble, and he helped her guard her secret. He needed to protect her; that's why he didn't even tell his closest friends. He did it all for her. He's a fucking saint now.

The pity for this murderer practically falls off the pages and pools beside my feet as I continue reading.

All I feel is anger rising from within. I'm struggling to read on, but I owe it to Jenny to continue so I can defend her if asked. Why did he do those awful things to her? I doubt it was consensual. He admitted to having erotic sex with her, but he is getting help now. His current therapist was permitted to say in the interview that her client is making great progress and is not a threat to women and that all of his past actions were consensual.

His therapist sounds like a real quack.

The article goes on to paint Liam in a better light, and now the paper needs someone to blame. The police have no new leads, so they focus on my poor sweet aunt Jenny and the girl who cried wolf. Me.

How did I know those things? Does it even matter? It led them to a sexual predator, and in my opinion, a murderer, so what does it matter now? I can't keep going on. It's too painful. Sorry, Jenny. They had him and they let him go.

# CHAPTER 49

*Charlie*
*August 2012*

My heart feels like it's going to jump through my chest and land on the floor in front of me.

I gather everything up in one long swoop and drop everything back down on Jenny's desk. I'm having a hard time understanding what I'm looking at and there is a pounding in my head that won't stop. I run my hands through the contents again, trying to comprehend what I just uncovered.

The words are so hateful. Someone really hated Jenny, but why? What was Jenny doing that was so wrong to this person, and did this have something to do with her death? What if it really wasn't Liam and he is innocent, like the police say? I always suspected the investigation was tainted and they had it wrong when they cleared Liam, but what if they didn't mess up and these notes are from the real killer?

Or are they from Liam, and I was right? I don't know what to think anymore.

I push all the notes to the right of the desk and my tapes to the left side, where Jenny's tape recorder is still sitting since her death. I open up the recorder and find another tape inside. This one is labeled Cindy Evans—Session Five. It's normal for Jenny to tape her sessions, but I wasn't a patient, and what did she record that would have my name on it?

I take out Cindy's tape and put the cassette labeled Charlie's Sessions—One in the recorder.

I lean back into Jenny's brown leather chair, trying to muster up the courage to hit play. My body is lifeless as it molds to the leather chair, becoming one with it.

I can't do it. I just can't bring myself to press the dang button. My finger hovers over it, shaking. Just then the double beep of my parents' car door locking shakes me from my debate.

Shoot! My parents are home. I know it would be upsetting if they found me disturbing Jenny's things. That was the last thing I wanted to do to them, especially now that we may have some new evidence. I don't want to upset them until I have a chance to think things over, until I know a bit more. I don't want to get their hopes up again. I have to know what is on my tapes first, before we go to the police. I can't share this information just yet.

Quickly I gather all the original content back into the box and toss everything back under the floorboard and cover everything back up, leaving Jenny's house just how I found it.

"Crap!" I yell as I trip over Quinn's suitcase. Another reminder of yet another mystery. It has to stay here for now. I tuck it into the pantry, so I don't have to lug it over to my house. I will be back tomorrow. It will be fine. My parents won't notice it if they happen to look in the window.

I quietly sneak in through the backdoor of our house before my parents come in through the garage. Cautiously, I tiptoe up to my bedroom. Tonight isn't the night to chat with them. I'm more confused than ever and I'm drunk. I really don't want to show them this side of me. I can't worry them. I don't bother to turn on the lights and I stumble to my bed. I crawl in with my clothes still on and gawk blankly at the dark ceiling above. Thinking, wishing, and praying for answers as the room starts spinning.

The investigators obviously didn't find the loose floorboard that housed these appalling notes addressed to my aunt, or the Charlie tapes. If they did, I think we would have heard about them. If they meant nothing, they would probably be sitting somewhere in the Deschutes County cold-case room, collecting dust. These notes could have been the break they needed four years ago; her murderer is still out there and the police gave up. They let Liam go, and then they had nothing. It's four years later and they still have no leads. The cops never found any evidence in her house that they could use to charge Liam. They searched his home too and nothing. Everything was a dead end. Maybe this is what they needed. Perhaps these notes were the connection to Liam. The cops never believed me. The cops were angry that I led them toward an innocent man. They lectured me, and so did my parents. I gave them a solid lead and they were ungrateful. They wouldn't have known Liam existed if it weren't for me. What thanks did I get? None.

I have to know what is on the Charlie tapes before I go to the police. They will question why the notes were in the box and why they were under the floorboard hiding. Why did Jenny feel the need to hide them? I need to know what I'm dealing with before I go to the useless PD. They had full access to Jenny's house and they never found what was right under their feet. Literally.

I need to know what is on the tapes. Tomorrow can't come quick enough.

# CHAPTER 50

### *Charlie*
### *August 2012*

I wait for my parents to leave for work, then I sneak back over to the guest house. I move the table, pull the rug back, and pry the floorboard back open. I'm almost afraid everything will be gone when I look back inside. I'm relieved to see everything is as I left it last night. I can't handle any more surprises.

Tightly gripping the fateful box, I pace the room, debating with myself. Should I listen to the tapes? What good is it going to do if I hear something that Jenny never intended for me to hear? On the other hand, if my tapes weren't a big deal, then why would they be hidden in the floor? Jenny could have easily just have placed them with her other patients' files. There is something I'm not supposed to know.

If I listen to the tapes, will I have more questions? Jenny isn't here to give me any answers.

It seems like everything I do lately ends in more unanswerable questions. It's like getting caught in a spider web; the more I move, the more wrapped up I get. I'm trapped.

The tapes. The box. The notes. Liam. Quinn. Asher. Jenny. My personal hell.

I have to know. OK, just the first tape. I can find out what I'm dealing with, then I can decide if I should continue. I place the small cherrywood box of secrets down on Jenny's desk. The first cassette is shaking in my hands as I push it into the recorder. Here we go. Pandora's box has been opened. I can't unhear what is on this tape. I bring my finger up to push play before I have a chance to change my mind.

Nothing. Static. Papers moving on the desk echo through the recording.

A hushed, whispered voice speaks. It's Jenny. A chill runs down my spine. I've missed her sweet voice so much. It hurts.

*"The date is April thirtieth, 2008."*

Tears rush down my face as I hear Jenny's sweet, calm voice.

*"Charlie has fallen asleep. I'm going to try a natural approach to hypnotherapy,"* Jenny says with her voice lowering.

I wiggle in the chair. My feelings from just moments ago of longing to hear her voice shift to a different emotion of confusion. Why would Jenny do this? Maybe she needed to test out hypnotherapy for one of her clients and if she told me about it, it wouldn't work? Maybe I was just part of a study for her. That must be it. Maybe she was going to tell me later, but never got the chance because someone took her life before she could.

*"Charlie, are you awake?"* Jenny's soft voice whispers. The sound of papers rustling and then static again projects from the recorder. *"Charlie, I need you to hear me."*

My own sleepy voice enters the room. *"Eh? Go away. I'm sleeping."*

I don't remember any of this. Is she in my bedroom? I don't remember falling asleep at her house. I feel violated. She has to be in my room. It's a very eerie feeling hearing your own voice saying words you don't remember.

Jenny continues. *"I'm going to need you to take a long, deep breath. Fill your lungs up. Keep your eyes closed but follow along. I know you are sleepy and that's OK. Follow my voice. Let your breath out and now breathe in another long breath."*

A long pause of dead air on the tape.

*"And now let it out. OK, good. Your eyes are heavy. Let all your muscles relax from your toes to your ears. You will feel relaxed now. Imagine your eyes getting heavier. Can you raise your hand for me?"* Another pause. *"OK good, now lower it."*

*"I'm going to need you to count backward from one hundred with me,"* Jenny says soothingly.

I obey. *"One hundred, ninety-nine, ninety-eight, ninety-seven . . ."*

Jenny counts down with me, repeating each number after I do. *"Ninety-four, ninety-three. Watch as each number disappears. Watch it float away. Eighty-eight, eighty-seven . . ."*

This is strange.

My counting continues down to eighty. And I stop.

*"Charlie, can you hear me?"* Jenny asks.

*"Yes."*

*"Can we talk about what has been bothering you?"* Jenny asks directly, but with concern hovering in her voice.

Bothering me? What is she talking about?

This is not about her patients; this is about me. What the hell?

*"No,"* I say.

*"Charlie, I'm going to ask you a series of questions, and I want you to answer them. OK?"* Jenny pauses. *"Are you worried about college at*

*Oregon State?"*

*"No. "*

*"Are you excited about college, then?"*

*"I'm just excited to leave, but I wish he could come with me. Maybe he could transfer. "*

Oh, my gosh. Am I talking about Liam to Jenny? My secret.

*"Who is he, Charlie? Who are you talking about?"* Jenny asks.

*"My boyfriend. "*

I'm shocked at the ease with which my secrets vacate my mouth without my will. I'm stunned by the betrayal from Jenny. Why couldn't she just have asked me about all of this? Why did she feel the need to do this in such a sneaky way?

*"I didn't know you had a boyfriend. Who is your boyfriend?"* Jenny asks nicely, although I'm sure she's dying to shake me awake and demand I tell her my secrets.

*"He is my . . ."* My voice trails off.

A loud noise interrupts the tape. Perhaps a car backfiring or something. Either way, it sounds like it ended my session. The static on the tape stops.

I leave the tape playing. A few moments of silence, and then Jenny's voice fills the air again. She is louder this time. I suspect she was in my room when she taped the session, and now, she is sitting in her office, just as I presently am. Sitting at her large oak desk in this very leather chair. I feel like I'm sitting on a ghost now.

*"Session One with Charlie Faye. "*

*Charlie took to hypnotherapy quickly. She was open to answering questions without too much prying. Hypnotherapy is worth trying again until we get to the underlying cause of her panic attacks. "*

Panic attacks? What is she talking about? I never had any panic attacks.

She continues. *"We were interrupted by a noise outside that broke her trance-like state. Next session, find out who she thinks her boyfriend is. Maybe she is confused with a movie or book she is reading. She never leaves the house, so having a real boyfriend seems unlikely. Perhaps an online boyfriend? I will look into her browser history. Proceed with second session."*

What other sneaky questions do you have for me in tape two, Jenny? You sneaky bitch.

# CHAPTER 51

### Charlie
### August 2012

Again, Jenny's voice fills the air the moment that I press play on tape two. *"The date is May ninth, 2008."*

She goes through the same routine with putting me into my hypnotic state. I'm in shock now as I listen. I'm not even sure what emotions to feel anymore. I have gone through sadness, anger, and fear all in one day. I feel like I'm going to explode. I try to focus on my breathing as I listen, but it's hard when I feel so much betrayal.

*"Ninety, eighty-nine, eighty-eight . . ."*

*"Charlie, can you hear me?"* Jenny asks soothingly and in a hushed voice.

*"No."*

*"Well, you responded. Can you hear me now?"*

*"Sure."*

*"OK. So, you have a boyfriend now. Do you want to tell me about him?"* Jenny asks.

*"No,"* I respond.

*"Why not?"*

*"You know why."*

My voice sounds different from what it did on the last tape. I seem almost angry and very agitated. Why the change?

*"No, I don't know why. Can you tell me why?"* Jenny asks.

*"Nope."*

*"Why not?"* Jenny says with calmness in her voice, pressing me to answer.

*"Because you know why."*

Wow. My sass. This doesn't sound like me. I'm actually a little freaked out, like I'm in a horror film and my head is going to do a 360 and snakes are going to pop from my head. What is going on with me?

*"I'm sorry, I don't know why you can't tell me, Charlie. Can you elaborate on why you're feeling this way?"* Jenny says, sounding so professional.

Silence and then static rips through the speaker.

*"No. Mind your own business."*

*"OK, that is fine. We don't have to talk about that right now. How are things with your friends?"*

*"Not great."*

*"Can we talk about that?"*

*"No."*

*"OK. How are you feeling right now?"*

*"Angry."*

*"Who are you angry with at school? A teacher? Mike or Zoey?"*

I'm dying to know who I'm angry with. I have to be dreaming. She must be pulling answers from my dreams. I was sleeping when she rudely interrupted my thoughts. That has to be it, just dreams. Sure, my friends were annoying me, but I don't think I would have chosen the word angry.

*"It's not at school. Don't worry about it. OK."*

A long pause.

*"Maybe he can transfer with me so he will forget about her. I saw them together, you know? He doesn't love her. She is a fucking slut!"*

My heart plummets to my feet. Why would I say that? Who did I see together? I'm even more convinced that it is all just a dream or perhaps a nightmare that she is pulling my so-called memories from. I couldn't have known about . . . No.

*"You know he hasn't shared with me much since he met her. I will get him back, and she will be gone. I will win."*

*"Who are you talking about? Where will she go?"* Jenny asks. Her voice is anxious. I can tell my words have shaken her. They shook me. They have no meaning to me either, Jenny.

*"She will just go away. Don't worry about it."*

A loud, untamed laugh erupts from the tape. A high-pitch evil laugh, the kind you hear in movies. Is that me? I've never laughed like that before. That couldn't be me. Goosebumps run up and down my entire body. Is it possible to be disturbed by your own self? Oh my gosh.

The recording pauses.

Just like the last tape, Jenny's voice enters again with her post-session notes.

*"I'm frightened by this session. Charlie wasn't acting like herself. She says she is angry with someone. Who? I still haven't seen her leave the house much except to go to school. Again, unknown who her boyfriend could be. Maybe it's a boy she sees only at school. I wonder if she is confused with a book she is reading. Sometimes people get caught up in a book or television show, thinking it's real life. They create an obsession with an alternate experience that never happened, but it feels real to them. Almost a state of delusion. Sadly, this tends to happen more in lonely people who avoid or have a hard time making friends or struggle to create genuine connections. I will have to*

*look around her room and see what books she is reading and what movies or TV shows she has been watching. I still need to check her browser history. She used the word slut, which is not in her regular vocabulary. Continue with hypnotherapy."*

The sound of three long claps makes me leap from my seat. The noise is out of place.

Was that on the tape?

Three more slow but long claps echo through the house. Not from the tape. It's coming from inside the house right now.

My eyes have to be playing tricks on me. It just can't be . . .

"How are you here?"

# CHAPTER 52

## Charlie
### August 2012

"How are you here?" I repeat my question.

"Well, you didn't leave me any options. I had to come get my shit, didn't I? Wasn't that all part of your plan?"

Quinn is standing in the doorway. In my fucking doorway. How? Why?

"Quinn!" I shout. "Thank God you're OK, but what the hell happened to you? Where were you and why have you been lying to me?" I stand up from my chair, pushing it up against the wall.

I'm grateful to see my so-called friend is OK, but I'm angry at the same time. She lied to me.

Quinn doesn't respond. I watch as she struts into the house. She flips her perfect blonde hair behind her shoulders and takes a seat on Jenny's couch. She looks untouched. Unruffled. Pretty and perfect. Not one scratch on her. I glance down at my arms, which are slowly healing.

I don't give her but a moment before I leap back into my

questioning. "Do you know I reported you missing, Quinn? I didn't know what else to do?"

"Charlie, you shouldn't have done that," Quinn says disapprovingly. She looks at me with a pouty face, her bottom lip sticking out further than the top. I can't help but notice her lip gloss. She had time to get ready and put herself together. She doesn't seem like a woman who was missing or in danger.

"What did you expect me to do? You weren't returning any of my phone calls and you never came back to the hotel," I shout.

"Charlie, Charlie, Charlie, I thought you would have understood things better by now, but my dear, sweet friend you just won't take a hint." Quinn laughs as she crosses her legs and resituates herself on the couch. She pulls a decorative pillow over her lap and gets even more comfortable.

"I don't understand," I scream.

"Oh, Charlie. You never understand."

"What is that supposed to mean? You're not making any sense right now. I demand you answer me. Why are you lying to me, Quinn?" I plead.

"I'm not the one lying, Charlie."

"Quit the games, Quinn. Just tell me what the fuck is going on!" I say, pounding my fist against the desk. It stings all the way down my hand and up my forearm to my elbow.

"So, this is Jenny's place, huh, Charlie." Quinn says, more in the form of a statement rather than a question.

"How do you know about Jenny? I never told you about her."

Quinn ignores the question. "Ah, yes the infamous Aunt Jenny. The super aunt who could do no wrong." Quinn's words slice through me, cutting my soul in half. I fall back into my chair; I want to wither down to the ground and hide under the desk.

"Tell me now! Where were you? Who are you? And how the

hell do you know anything about Jenny?" I scream.

Quinn gets up from the couch. She isn't fazed by my outburst. She calmly walks around the room. I'm shaking; vibrating. I feel rage rising from my feet, rushing up my entire body. Quinn continues to slowly walk the length of the room until she is right in front of me, hovering over the big oak desk. She stares me directly in the eye, and then I watch her eyes change direction and move toward a picture on the desk. She points at the photo on the desk.

"Charlie, is this Mrs. Perfect Aunt Jenny?" Quinn says in a sinister voice. She picks up a framed photo of my mom and Jenny that was taken the year before Jenny died. I know the photo well. We have the same one framed in our house. It's my mom's favorite picture of Jenny.

"Yes, and that's my mom," I respond with my head down. A tear rolls down my cheek. I don't want Quinn to see that she is really hurting me right now, although I suspect that is her intent, but why? Who would do the things this girl has done to a friend?

A malicious smile spreads across her face and her brow furrows. "Interesting. She is quite beautiful, like me, wouldn't you agree?"

Narcissistic much, Quinn?

"Your mom is a little old-looking, though, but still pretty. Do you think she was ever jealous of Jenny? Were you ever jealous of Jenny? It's clear that Auntie was definitely the prettiest one in this family. Wouldn't you agree? I'm mean, look at her. She's hot! Her long, thick brown hair, and dang look at that smile. Tall and skinny. The perfect female specimen. I bet all the guys flocked to her. How are you even related to her? I just don't see it," Quinn says all of this so casually, but she knows she is getting under my skin.

"What is your point, Quinn? Can't you just knock it off? You're really hurting me. Don't you care about me?"

"Yes, I care about you, Charlie. Why do you think I'm here? I think, it's time you play the last tape. You know that little box with the tapes labeled 'Charlie's Sessions.'"

I just found them yesterday. How could she possibly know that?

"Are you stalking me? Have you been watching me? I've been so worried, and you've been here the whole goddamn time!" I shout at her.

Quinn has a smug look on her face, and she starts twirling her hair around her fingers. "Hey Charlie, why don't you pop in that last tape? Let's take a listen together, shall we?"

"What! No! I don't understand. Get out of my house," I demand.

"Don't you mean Jenny's house?" Quinn taunts.

"I mean it—I'm going to call the cops! Leave now," I say sternly, pointing toward the door.

"I wouldn't do that if I were you, Charlie. OK, let's forget about the tape for a second and let's talk about the night I left. Do you remember what happened in Iowa, Charlie?"

I sadly shake my head.

"Because I do, Charlie. I remember it all."

# CHAPTER 53

### Charlie
### August 2012

"Quinn, I'm sick of your games," I shout.

"I think you might want to wait on kicking me out of Jenny's house until we get to the bottom of things. Don't cha think? We have a lot to talk about. Tell me what you remember about our last night in Iowa together."

I don't know why, but I humor her. I need answers, and if this is how I'm going to get them, then whatever. I guess I have to play along with Quinn's little game.

"I honestly only remember the day after the party, when you and Nash were packing your things. I remember waking up with the flavor of death in my mouth because I drank too much. I knew something happened because I could feel it in my bones, but I couldn't put the pieces together."

"Keep going, Charlie. I need you to unravel this on your own. You need to get it this time."

"This time?" I question.

"Keep the memory rolling. Charlie."

"Don't you think I've been trying this entire summer? No thanks to you, I might add. How could you just leave and not have the decency to at least tell me what the piss I did?" I shout at her.

"Charlie, it will all make sense. I just need you to work through this," Quinn responds with authority.

She moves back over to the couch, like she is getting ready for a night of girl talk. She sits cross-legged in the middle. But I'm still ready to pounce. I can't sit down. I'm too upset. How is she so blasé about all of this?

"Keep going. What else do you remember?" Quinn presses me to continue.

"You just had to have your year-end bash. Didn't you? If we could have just ordered pizza and watched a movie as I suggested, none of this would have happened, whatever the hell it was that I did. But honestly, all I remember is stumbling out of my room, looking for medicine because I felt like I had gotten hit by a semi-truck."

"Yah, Charlie. Side note—I think you have a drinking problem, but that's the least of your quandaries right now. We will address that one later," Quinn says.

I give her a snide look. "Anyway, I walk into the kitchen and I'm shocked and saddened to see you and Nash quietly sneaking around, packing all your things, and moving out of our apartment. Our fucking home for four years. You already had packing tape and boxes. Like, where the hell did all that come from? You must have started hours before I caught you, and when you saw me, you had that deer-in-the-headlights look. You didn't plan for me to wake up. Did you? You looked like the guilty one, Quinn."

Quinn doesn't speak but instead motions with the sign for "let's get the show on the road."

Bitch.

"But I did catch you and I asked why, and you didn't give me a response. Nash kept his head down and kept packing your things. Before I knew it, you were both outside with Nash's truck full of our memories."

"OK, thanks for the recap, but that is everything you already knew. We need to dive into that night, and what you don't remember."

"No shit, Sherlock. That's what I'm trying to do," I say to her sarcastically. I'm getting frustrated with this stupid game. "Just tell me," I shout.

"Charlie, do you remember the Jenny drawer? Think about it, do you remember me on your bed trying to talk you down?"

"Talk me down?" I question.

"Think hard and pull from deep in your memory. You have it. It is there," Quinn says.

"I . . . I remember I had too much to drink," I stutter as I close my eyes, trying hard to put the pieces back together from that night. "Nash bought a lot of beer for the party and I had too much to drink. I remember feeling sad about leaving college, about leaving you. I now vaguely remember finding you sitting on my bed.

"What did you do when you saw me, Charlie?"

"I don't remember, Quinn."

"Yes, you do!" Quinn shouts

"I just, um, I just remember you were going through things in my Jenny drawer. Wait! Is that how you knew about Jenny just now? Because you were in my drawer that night."

"Keep going, Charlie, you're almost there."

"I remember you going through my drawer and pulling out all of Jenny's pictures. You had everything laid out across my bed.

Every picture, every memory I had with Jenny. I was mad that
you touched my things, my secret things."

I'm enraged now. I want to cry. I'm surprised I remembered that.

Quinn keeps pressing me for more, but I can't find anything
else. No other memory is coming back from that night.

"Charlie, that is when I told you the truth and you didn't want
to hear it."

I sit with a quizzical look on my face. "I don't understand."

"Maybe we should just play the last tape, Charlie. You're just
not getting it," Quinn says, disappointed in my lack of memory.

"Remind me again, where the hell you were the past two days,
and when did you start watching me?" I demand.

She ignores me again and leaps to her feet, joining me back
at the desk. Before I can grab the tape, she has it in her hand.
"Charlie, I wish it didn't have to be this way, but here we go. You
have to know the truth," Quinn says, shaking the tape in my face.

"That is all I've been asking for this whole dang time. The
truth," I scream.

Quinn places the tape in the recorder. Then with her perfectly
manicured hand she pushes down hard on the green triangle
button of Jenny's old tape recorder. "Well, be careful what you
wish for."

# CHAPTER 54

## Charlie
## August 2012

The start of the third tape is different than the first two. *"The date is May twenty-forth, and I'm afraid."* Jenny is speaking louder when she states the date. I suspect she taped that part at her desk. The tape doesn't have Jenny putting me into the trance. She must have forgotten to push record. When the tape resumes, Jenny's voice is shaky. *"Charlie, can you hear me?"*

I really don't want to listen to this now, especially with Quinn staring at me. I want to push stop, but I doubt Quinn is going to let that happen. I sit back in my chair and listen involuntarily and against my will.

My words fill the room, and I sit back in my chair. No point in trying to get Quinn to stop.

*"No, I can't hear you."*

Obviously, I heard her if I answered.

*"Can you hear me now?"* Jenny asks again.

*"Yes! What do you want?"*

My words hiss from my mouth, cold and unfriendly. You can hear me taking a deep breath and a quick huff out. Jenny must have the recorder close to my body on my bed. I feel violated again.

Jenny asks, *"Are you still dating your boyfriend?"*

*"Wouldn't you like to know?"*

*"I would like to know, that is why I'm asking, Charlie,"* Jenny presses me.

*"I'm so angry. She betrayed us."*

*"Who are you angry with, Charlie, and who is us?"*

*"I wanted him to be the one, but he cheated. I don't think he knows that I know. We can fix this, but she can't be here anymore. He loves me, and she was just the slut that teased him. I don't think she ever loved him. Maybe I should hurt him too. I know it's not his fault, though. It's hers."*

*"Who are you talking about?"* Jenny demands.

*"I fucking hate her—she is such a whore. I want her to feel the pain she made me feel. I feel like my heart is being torn from my chest. They hurt me badly. She needs to pay for what she did. I can't believe what I saw."* My voice gets louder with each sentence.

I hear soft sobs from the tape. Are they mine or Jenny's? I can't tell.

*"My friend told me I can't talk about it anymore."*

*"Charlie, who is your friend?"*

*"My friend said she is a nasty bitch."*

*"Can I meet your friend?"* Jenny asks.

*"You will meet her soon."*

"Those words don't feel like mine. I'm so scared and confused, Quinn."

Quinn presses stop on the recorder and hands me a folded-up piece of paper that she pulled from her pocket. "This was in the Jenny drawer. You need to read it."

# CHAPTER 55

### Charlie
### August 2012

Quinn hands me the paper and I unfold it. It's an old newspaper article.

*Liam Sutter's Innocence Proven by Northern California Couple.*

An image of Liam smiling with an elderly couple in front of his sage-green house on that stupid familiar street stares me directly in the face. They have a pile of photographs in their hand.

I want to vomit.

"Charlie, do you remember this article?" Quinn asks.

"No, I don't," I respond.

"It was mixed in with your things in the Jenny drawer in your nightstand. You need to read it," Quinn says, pressing me to continue.

*Many questions surrounded the recent release of Liam Sutter as the main suspect in the murder of psychologist Dr. Jenny Morrison, but Sutter has a Northern California couple to thank for his removal from the suspect list.*

*Margaret and Saul Bowerman were sitting in their home when they saw the news about a homicide investigation surrounding a murder that happened in May. Margaret recalls almost fainting when Liam's photo appeared as the main suspect in Morrison's death. "We just got back from spending a summer camping in our RV. We hadn't seen or heard any news in months. We were just shocked when we heard a poor woman had been murdered the same day we were camping in that very town. We were even more shocked when the man they suspected as the murderer was Liam. After putting together the timeline, we knew it couldn't have been this man. We spent the entire day with him. There was no way he would have killed that poor girl, and we had evidence to prove it."*

*Sutter was always firm and stuck to his alibi that he was camping with his sister and niece just outside of town the morning Jenny was murdered, although Sutter's sister couldn't confirm that Liam was at the campsite at the time of Morrison's death—she had had to leave in the middle of the night with her toddler as it was too cold for her and the child was getting fussy. Liam always stated he met a couple that could confirm his innocence, but police could never locate the so-called couple and no one else ever came forward to substantiate his story. The police assumed he was lying, and it made him look even more guilty. He couldn't remember their names or any other identifying details.*

*According to Saul Bowerman, he was just sick to his stomach over this because he had proof he was with the suspect and he felt bad he hadn't seen the news earlier. "We saw Liam attempting to light a campfire the morning of the girl's murder. He was struggling because the wood was wet. He wasn't going to get anything going with that wet stuff, so my wife and I invited him over to our fire and we enjoyed breakfast together. We had enough for all of us. He seemed like a nice* young lad. We told Liam that we were photographers, and he spent the entire day asking me questions—he told us he was an aspiring photographer too. We enjoyed his company. He stayed and played cards with us all day and picked my brain about cameras, exposures, and nature photography. My wife took photos of us throughout the day and luckily, they were date stamped. We don't condone the kind of relationship Liam had with the girl, but we couldn't let an innocent man go to prison for something he truly didn't do. We hope he continues to get the help he needs."

To remind our readers how Sutter came to be the main suspect in Morrison's murder, we have to go back to how his name was falsely given to the police. Morrison's niece, Charlie Faye, gave his name to the police but never revealed any evidence to support her suspicion. Also, she could not explain how she knew Sutter was the man responsible for the murder. Sources close to the case say Faye was shocked by her own outburst and didn't remember saying his name after she shouted it to the police.

Later it came out that Faye admitted to being in a relationship with Sutter. This, of course, shifted the investigators' attention to Faye herself. Did she have motive to kill her aunt? If Liam was dating both girls, then one must have been jealous of the other. Liam denied all of that. He said he accidently went to the wrong house and met Faye once. That, according to Sutter, was the only contact he ever had with her and they never had the relationship that Faye claims.

This new information put Faye on top of the list of suspects, and they shifted their attention and efforts to her. Faye and Sutter both were given lie-detector tests, and both passed. Faye was eventually taken off the suspect list. Faye still holds strong to the fact that she *was involved with Sutter, and Sutter still claims he only met her once. The only part of their stories that matched up was the day they met, but they still both passed the lie detector. With no further evidence to link Faye to her aunt's murder, she was removed as a suspect.*

*Investigators have had no other leads to pursue. The family is losing hope that Jenny's killer will ever be caught.*

"Charlie, Liam didn't kill Jenny. You have to believe that part now," Quinn says with tenderness in her voice.

"I don't remember any of this, Quinn. I really don't. If police cleared me and Liam, then who did it? Who killed Jenny?"

# CHAPTER 56

## Charlie
## August 2012

I grab the four notes with one hand and shake them toward Quinn. "Who the hell killed my aunt and who wrote her these hateful notes? I don't get what you're trying to get out of me, Quinn? I just don't understand."

Quinn ignores me and presses play again on the tape recorder.

Once again, Jenny's quivery voice fills the air. The hairs on my arm stand erect, and goosebumps quilt my entire body. I instantly feel queasy and unsure I want to continue listening, but Jenny's words continue, and I'm stuck, paralyzed in my chair.

*"I'm afraid of what I heard and saw tonight in Charlie's room. I finally was able to see her computer and what I found in her browser history, well, frankly terrifies me. I had hoped it was a book or TV show influencing her, but it's much worse than I could have ever predicted. I feel ill.*

*Liam Sutter, Liam Sutter, Liam Sutter. Liam Sutter. Every single drop-down in her history had his name somewhere in the search.*

*Myspace—Liam Sutter. Photography—Liam Sutter. Facebook—Liam*

*Sutter*

*I'm dumbfounded as to how she even knows him. I'm scared if she really does have a relationship with this monster. Could he be doing the same things to her that he did to me? Could he be tormenting her too? I'm so confused but I think she believes she is dating Liam, and perhaps they are dating, but I'm not sure what to think. She says she has a boyfriend, and she is quite jealous of the other woman he is seeing.*

*Me.*

*She wants to harm that person.*

*Me.*

*If Charlie weren't my niece, I would . . ."*

Jenny trails off. She takes a deep sigh and then resumes.

*"What kind of predator did I bring into our lives?*

*I will have to go to the police tomorrow to report what Liam did to me. I can't continue to let him get away with what he's doing, even if that means I have to blow up my own life in doing so. I can't let him harm another person, especially not my sweet Charlie. He's done a number on her psyche, whether they are dating or not. She is clearly obsessed with this awful man. I will give her the respect of attending her graduation tomorrow before I go to the police and before I fill in Joan and Frank on Charlie's hypnotherapy. This will break their hearts. She has been withdrawn from the family, her friends, and school, and if she isn't dating Liam, I have to think about the possibility of delusional thinking."*

Jenny chokes back tears.

*"Oh my. It couldn't be—Mom. Just like Mom . . . Did Joan know? She told me to think about Mom. Is this what she meant? Was I blind to what I didn't want to see? Look into schizophrenia, post-traumatic stress disorder, or dissociative identity disorder, but refer her for further evaluation. I cannot confirm at this time. I also cannot continue to treat her after today. This will be my last session with Charlie."*

Static again.

Then Jenny's voice enters once again.

*"Charlie must have seen me and Liam together. What if Charlie is the one writing me the notes? Did she see Liam at my house today? What did she see? What if. . . Oh, my God. It has to be her, who else could it be?"*

Jenny starts crying on the tape and it echoes through the house, bouncing off every wall and hitting me right in my heart. The tape stops.

"Charlie, why do you think her screams haunt you at night?"

"I don't know, I don't know, Quinn," I say with fear, tears streaming down my face. "How do you know all of this, Quinn?"

"Think about it, Charlie. Remember the rest of the party? You were so confused. You were beyond inebriated, and you started pacing the room. Back and forth. Back and forth, mumbling to yourself after you saw all the Jenny memories spread out on the bed. You went back out to the party where you confronted Nash. You called him Liam and said he was cheating on you with Jenny. Does any of this ring a bell now?"

"Why would I care what Nash was doing, and why would I have been so confused?" I cry.

"You started hyperventilating as you paced the room. We couldn't get you to calm down. Nash tried getting you to breathe, and you wouldn't sit still long enough for us to help you. You were chewing on your fingernails and pacing and breathing heavily in a panic for what felt like hours but was probably a matter of only fifteen minutes. We couldn't get you to stop. Suddenly, you snapped and jumped on Nash. You pushed him to the ground and started slapping him repeatedly. You called him Liam and told him to get off Jenny. You were a scrappy little fighter, and he couldn't push you off without hurting you, so he just took it. You repeatedly called him Liam. Nash kept screaming at you, demanding who Jenny and Liam were. I just sat there afraid to speak or do anything. Charlie, that's why we left. You were out of your mind, and we were afraid of you. You were so confused, and Nash couldn't get you to explain yourself. Eventually, you tired yourself out, and we put you to bed. Nash shut the party down. Most people cleared out on their own after your drunken antics. He started packing immediately after. Charlie, I tried to show you the truth, but I couldn't help. I had to leave."

No, no. I feel dizzy. This isn't right. Quinn is lying.

"Go screw yourself and get out of my house," I shout.

"You came over to Jenny's house when she left for her run the morning she died. Charlie, you wrote that last note for her, but Jenny didn't see your warning, did she? 'The pretty ones deserve what they get, the pretty ones deserve to die.' You wrote that Charlie. You followed her and you took that ugly stuffed-toy monkey with you. The one with the heart that Liam gave her. You did that, Charlie. How else would you know she screamed?"

"I still don't understand—"

"You were there. You fucking killed Jenny, Charlie."

# CHAPTER 57

*Charlie*
*August 2012*

"I need you to say it out loud. I need you to remember," Quinn shouts at me, but I'm already out the door.

I take off, running from Quinn. I cross the yard and dash into my house, up the stairs, and into my bedroom. I close the door behind me. I latch the lock shut. I pound my fist against the door.

"Charlie," Quinn's voice whispers behind me. I jump.

"Are you kidding me, how are you here right now? You can't be here. How did you get in here?"

I close my eyes, and when I open them, Quinn is still there. Sitting on my bed.

"Charlie, come have a seat next to me. I want you to lay down on the bed," Quinn says in a calm, soothing voice. I obey her. She runs her fingers through my hair.

"Shhh. Be quiet and calm your body down. I need you to relax. I need you to be still. I need you to find that memory."

"Charlie. I think it's time you remember what happened."

# CHAPTER 58

*Charlie*
*May 2008*

I'm quiet these days. I sneak around, going unnoticed. I tiptoe through Jenny's life. She doesn't know I'm watching her. I watch Jenny and I follow Liam. I see what they do together when they think they're alone. But they are never really alone. I tried to leave notes to warn Jenny. It would have been so much easier if she had just listened, but she couldn't leave him alone. She is a slut. I watched the things they did together. I sat outside her window. I narrated the things I couldn't hear. He twisted into what she needed from him. She made him do things to her—that is not the Liam I know. The Liam I know is sweet, kind, and loves his family and friends. Jenny made him into a sex-crazed monster. I tried to stay outside and watch, but sometimes I would go inside and get a closer look.

Yesterday, he showed up with flowers and a stuffed animal. His act is making me sick. I'm so mad at them. How could they do this to me? Those flowers should be for me. Not her.

Jenny is a lying whore. I can't believe I trusted her. She knew that what she was doing was wrong. She shouldn't have seduced her patient. My Liam. She is so old compared to him too. He is closer to my age. Liam and I make sense, not her and Liam.

I let myself into her house when she is in the shower. I leave her one final warning.

*To Jenny, the nasty slut whore who ruined my life,*
*The pretty ones deserve what they get. The pretty ones deserve to die.*

Feeling very satisfied with my threat, I swirl around in her office chair, chuckling to myself, careful not to alert Jenny. I can't tell if I mean my threat or if it is just to scare her. Only time will tell, I guess. After all, Jenny deserves this scare. Nothing else seems to be getting through her thick skull. The thought of her reading this gives me a jolt of excitement. I feel so in control of this situation, of everything. I love this feeling. This feeling of power makes me want more of it.

Jenny has no idea I am in her home while she is showering. I feel compelled to act on my newfound power. I touch everything in her house. I look through drawers, quietly, of course. I dive headfirst into her life. The thrill calms for a moment when I find a set of tapes labeled Charlie's Sessions. What the heck are these?

Jenny's shower turns off. I will have to come back for the tapes later. I know I'm playing recklessly and taking risks. I stay for a few more minutes. I peek around the corner and see Jenny lacing up her running shoes, sitting on the edge of her bed, facing the window. I know where she is going. I'm always one step ahead of Jenny.

I yank the stuffed monkey from the counter and shove it into the pocket of my black hoodie.

I head back outside and pace the yard, waiting for her to leave. I feel the rage and anger setting back in.

Once I see her take off running. I get in my car and I wait on the other side of the river for her to arrive. She is taking longer than I expected. This is her favorite spot to run. She has to come here. A jolt of excitement rushes through my body when I see her running up to the trail. Just as I planned. She runs on one side of the river, while I run on the other. Just me and her and a river in between us.

I want her to feel safe, so I stay a little behind her pace. She can't see me just yet. I keep a watchful eye on her. Her brown ponytail flaps behind her with each bounce in her step. About a quarter of a mile into the trail, it's time to play a little game. I throw my hood up over my head. Slip into my black gloves and increase my speed. She notices me right away from across the river. She slows down. I slow down. She picks up her pace. I match it. Oh, dear Jenny, I'm your worst nightmare. Your instincts are correct. I am watching you. She speeds up again. I back off for a moment and she lets her guard down again. I see her stopping for breath at the top of her incline. I hurry to get to her before she runs again. I stand along the riverbank; I'm below her view so she can't see who I am. I keep my head down and rock joyously on the heels of my feet, back and forth. I just can't resist. I slowly bring my gloved hand up, twiddling each finger, starting with my pinky. It's so eerie, I give myself chills. I grin in the knowledge that I have shaken her to her core. I can't see her face, but I know panic is conjuring across it. I feel a sick satisfaction that I've never felt before. I feel alive; I feel different. My entire body tingles in fulfillment.

I can't completely scare her off. I'm not done yet. I double back so she thinks I'm leaving. I need her to feel safe again. It's time for her to let her guard down. Once I see her in the distance,

I increase my pace and make myself a new trail so she can't see me. I'm surprisingly fast and light on my feet. I continuously flash through the forest, maintaining an eye on Jenny, but she would never see me, because Jenny wouldn't even think to look for me here.

I'm always one step ahead, literally this time. I'm smarter than Jenny and faster; I have to be. My new path is a faster, flatter route than the original trail. I make it to the bridge before Jenny. I can still see her coming in the distance. She slows down her pace since she thinks her threat has left. The river is rushing faster and is deeper than downstream, flowing just below the bridge with little room to spare. It is just me, Jenny, and the river. Not another soul in sight. I spot a rather generous tree to hide behind. I peek around the trunk, careful not to expose myself to my aunt. She thoughtfully approaches the bridge. Once she assesses that no threat is near, she makes her way to the middle.

Jenny faces forward, so I take the opportunity to sneak quietly behind her.

She looks a little too peaceful for my taste—time to disturb that.

The bridge sways the second my foot hits the wooden planks as I hear Jenny whisper to herself, "I wish I could stay here forever."

Perfect idea, Jenny. I jolt her to the ground and reply to her rhetorical question. "Oh, pretty, pretty, Jenny, you can stay here forever."

Jenny screams.

I'm now straddling her body, one foot on each side of her. My weight, which isn't much, is keeping Jenny pinned down. I center my foundation on the midsection of her back in an attempt to keep her stomach pressed firmly into the wood, making it harder for her to free herself. I twist her long, thick brown ponytail in my hand and use it as leverage to keep her face pinned down.

"Jenny, Jenny, Jenny. What am I going to do with you?" I taunt.

Jenny screams as she tries to free herself. Her shoulders twist from side to side, and she thrusts her feet rapidly. The bridge sways with each movement.

"Oh, does this hurt?" I laugh.

Jenny's head twists just enough to get a look at my face with her left eye.

I use my free hand to twist her face back toward the planks of the bridge. I give it a nice little upward push, hoping she will get some splinters in that pretty little face of hers.

"Charlie, why?" Jenny sputters out.

"Oh, Jenny, you fucking slut, you know why."

Jenny pleads again as her face scrapes up and down as she tries to struggle free.

"Why, Charlie, why would you do this to me? I love you. We're family."

"Jenny, family would never do what you did," I speak to her patronizingly. "You are sick and fucked in the head. Liam is mine. Did you know that? You took him from me and made him do all those foul things to you. I know, I watched you time and time again. I was always there, Jenny. I saw everything you and Liam did. You are sick. You ruined him, and things will never be the same."

"Charlie, you need help," Jenny said, trying to sound convincing.

I interrupt her. "Help? What from Dr. Jenny? Lucky you won't be around much longer to continue to fuck up your patients like you did with Liam."

Jenny shakes again underneath me, trying to free herself as she pleads for me to release her. "Charlie, get off me, and I can explain everything to you. That's not what happened. How do you even know Liam? He isn't who you think he is. He hurt me.

Did you not see that? Please, Charlie. I love you."

"Jenny, none of that matters now." I release my left hand and reach into my sweatshirt pocket and pull out that stupid little monkey stuffed animal that Liam brought over last night. I tighten my grip on her hair and roll her entire body to face me. I press my butt into her stomach with all my weight and I shove the stuffed animal over her mouth.

Jenny's body thrusts and her arms swat toward my face. She tries to pull the toy away from her mouth. I shift my weight into my upper torso, and with all my might, I push harder into the soft creature. Jenny tries to puff for breath. The more she gasps, the harder it is for her to breathe. She is still panting, so I release one hand and wrap it tightly around her throat. Her entire body convulses under me. Shaking and gyrating from her head to her toes. Her stomach moves quickly up and down, and then the movements slow. I whisper softly into her ear, "Jenny, the pretty ones deserve what they get. The pretty ones deserve to die."

Her eyes roll back into her head, and her entire body flops, lifeless.

I pick up the stuffed animal and shove it back into my pocket. I pull her dense body to the end of the bridge and roll her into the river. Jenny's body catches between two rocks as the rapids flow over her. Her once vibrant brown locks are soaked and in a repetitional flow downstream.

Someone will find her soon.

As I walk off the bridge, I spot a homeless man leaning up against a tree. Oh fuck. Oh shit. I didn't think anyone was out here. Maybe he didn't see anything.

"Hey little girl, I saw what you did." He slurs his speech.

The old dirty man is drunk. He doesn't know what he's talking about. His smell is putrid, whiskey, cigarettes, and urine.

"Hey, little girl, get back here. You can't just leave that there."
He continues to shout at me, but I just walk away.

***

Back at Jenny's house, I gather my notes and the three tapes that are labeled Charlie's Sessions. It doesn't appear that she even opened my last note, and that was my best one too. Oh Jenny, you didn't even see me coming today. You didn't have the fear I hoped for, but it still worked out just fine. Well, just fine for me, that is.

Jenny already had a box with the same label in her drawer, ready to go. Oh, sneaky Jenny.

Oh shoot, the time, I am going to be late. I want to listen to the tapes, but I can't right now. I will come back for these later.

Where to hide the box? Ah, the loose floorboard. I noticed the table shake every time someone put a glass on it. I knew my observation would come in handy.

Sure enough, I'm able to wedge Jenny's letter opener under it and knock it looser. Loose enough for me to peel it back and safely tuck my precious box under it for no one but me to find. It will be safe here. I pull the rug back over it and put everything back in its proper place.

I skip back home.

Everything is going to be OK now.

# CHAPTER 59

### Charlie
### August 2012

"Why would you make me remember something so awful, Quinn? How could I have done that? I loved Jenny. I swear. I don't want that memory anymore. Take it back," I shout at Quinn.

"Yes, you loved and still have love in your heart for her, but, sweetie, you get confused. You get blinded, and you can't see what is real."

I'm lifeless, motionless, and my body is sinking into my bed. Quinn continues to stroke my hair.

"Charlie, you have always known the truth. I just have to help you remember from time to time. You block out things that you don't want to remember. You've been doing that your whole life. I need you to understand that your relationship with Liam wasn't real. Think back to your time at Coffee Loon. It was just you, two cups of coffee, and your laptop. You had a crush on Liam, a man you met once. You wanted it to be more than it could ever be so badly that you made it real in your head. Everything you knew about him, you found on the internet. Think about his Facebook posts."

*Going snowshoeing with the guys. Photos coming soon.*

*Photos from Europe. Just me, my backpack, and my trusty camera.*

*My brother-in-law lost his fight with cancer.*

*Pictures of my little Lily Pad.*

*Photo-editing class at 2 p.m.*

*Snowshoeing up Tumalo Mountain tomorrow with boards strapped to our packs. Action shots of Eric coming soon.*

"The photography you saw was what he posted on his social media, Charlie. His photos were everywhere on Facebook for you to see. He was not sitting in front of you. Just your computer."

Tears soak my face. I try hard to think back to my time with Liam.

"I'm sorry, Charlie, but that relationship just wasn't real."

Images flood back over me. I can see right through his spot at our table. It's just me, two coffees, my computer, and an empty chair.

"You're messing with my memories now," I cry.

"Sweetie, you got angry when Liam stopped posting," Quinn says. "He was in a secret relationship with Jenny, so he didn't share as much. You didn't have anything new to look at, so that made you angry, paired with the fact you saw them kissing in her bedroom that awful night. You tried to block it out, but your body and mind couldn't handle what you saw. You had a full-blown meltdown, followed by the panic attack. Whether you remember it or not, you stalked them and started leaving the notes for Jenny to find. You got a rise from it, didn't you, Charlie? Then remember seeing them with the handcuffs? Remember how that made you feel inside? But the truth is, Jenny was being hurt by this monster and all you saw was what you wanted to see. And you got it all wrong. You passed the lie-detector test with the investigators because you forgot the truth. You honestly thought you didn't have anything to do with it. You flipped a switch and blocked everything out the second you walked back into your house on graduation day. The lies—your new beliefs, they just started flying out of your mouth. It was like nothing happened. Charlie, you really believed you were living a nightmare where someone killed your aunt. You never went back for the box that contained all your secrets. You did have a slight slip when you spouted Liam's name to the police. You were so confused, but you didn't let yourself put the pieces together. Also, your alibi didn't hold up and that made you even more confused. You never had brunch with your friends. They didn't cover for you either, Charlie. Luckily, the cops didn't have enough evidence to charge you, and you believed your own lies so much that this lie proved to be real on the polygraph test. Mike didn't want anything to do with you, but sweet Zoey wanted to help you and understand. She called you over and over, but you never answered. Zoey eventually stopped trying. You're a good blocker, Charlie, but you need my help to remember. How do you feel about all this? Does it hurt deep down?"

I want to die. I can't breathe. I feel my body being weighted down into the bed.

"Quinn, can you stop please?" I cry.

"Remember this little guy?" Quinn says as she tosses the stuffed-toy monkey with the heart right at me. "The murder weapon has been sitting here on your papasan chair for the past four years."

Quinn looks at me, her face grave. "Charlie, we can't stop. You need to pull your shit together. We have to finish this time. Here, follow me back to Jenny's." She takes my hand and leads the way. I have no choice but to follow.

Back inside the guest house, Quinn pulls the suitcase from the pantry. "Open it, Charlie. These are not my clothes. They are Jenny's clothes that you packed yourself from Jenny's closet."

"No, that can't be. This is your suitcase, your clothes," I scream.

Quinn doesn't skip a beat and continues. "After your failed internship this summer, you came back here for a couple of days. It stirred things up inside you. You began to drink a lot. You wanted me again. You longed for our friendship that you shut out because I tried to remind you of the truth when I showed you the contents of your nightstand drawer. The Jenny drawer. But then you forgot and needed me again. You made the reservations at the hotel. You dressed yourself up."

I can't breathe. I can't think clearly. She is messing with me.

"Charlie, don't you get it now? You created me. Think about it, I showed up when you needed a friend. I always show up. I showed up in sixth grade when you bullied that little girl, Sophia."

"No, she bullied me, and I only met you four years ago," I shout to Quinn, defending myself.

"Charlie, remember you block out what you don't want to remember. Your parents know the truth. They know the kind of things you are capable of. They've always known you have a dark side that you can easily tuck away. You bullied that little girl so bad her family had to move. You scared little Sophia. The cute girl with freckles. Remember that now? Your parents never told Jenny, but they suspected Jenny would eventually figure you out, especially when she became a doctor. They were ready for it this time, but they didn't want you to tell your secrets to a stranger. They had Jenny now to help you, but Jenny was too blind to see what you were capable of until it killed her. If she only saw it coming sooner. She loved you too much to see your truth. Your grandma was sick too, just like you. It's probably genetic. She didn't get the help she needed. She drove her car off the road. Granny killed herself and your grandpa. At least that is what your mom suspects happened. You heard her and Jenny talking about it once. Your family sucks at getting people the help they need. Jenny really should have seen this coming sooner. She should've helped you. Some therapist she was."

None of this is real. I'm dreaming. I pinch my right hand with my left and I feel a teensy prick. Fuck.

"I taught you that little trick. Pinch yourself to see if it's real. Charlie, it's always real but you need a little reminder."

"I still don't understand how you know all of this. All of my secrets and all of my memories. You couldn't have been there."

"Charlie, I know, because you know."

"What?"

"I'm not real, Charlie! You created me in your head. Like I said earlier, I come out when you need me and always have. This time I was here longer, and you made me your new Jenny out of guilt.

I look like her. I'm pretty like her. You watch me do the things you want to do and then sometimes you pretend to be me. Don't you see now? Nash was your boyfriend, not mine, because I'm not real. You wanted him at the frat party. You used your new friend, me, to gain confidence and talk to him. It worked for you, but I'm not real. You are. Nash is, but I'm not. When I'm with you, you get more confidence, and you got a guy like Nash."

"What happened to Asher?" I ask with caution in my voice. Afraid to hear the truth.

"You were in Seattle. I wasn't with you. You got Asher all on your own, but then you started to get confused with him. You upped and left when he said he had to leave for San Francisco. You accused him of cheating. You found yourself back in Bend, back in your old habits and drinking again. He called to check in on you and tell you he was coming back to Portland. You made hotel reservations and brought your Jenny suitcase of clothes. You snuck out to meet him and got confused again. You guys fought, but he still came the next day to make sure you were OK. You freaked out on the poor guy again and when you ran away, he eventually came back to find you. You punched him in the nose and broke it. That's why you were covered in blood. You got scared, and you ran away and ended up in that random alley. And poor Asher probably ended up in the hospital."

Quinn stands directly in a ray of light, and it bounces off her perfect blonde hair. If she isn't real, then how come I can see her? How can she be here and continue to talk to me?

"I thought the detective in Portland shattered things for you when he said my phone number wasn't in use, but you took it to a new level and presumed I was lying. Look at your phone, Charlie. All those undelivered messages. You chose to see what you wanted."

I stare at Quinn. I have no words.

Quinn continues. "And the one person besides me who knows the truth, that poor drunk homeless man by the river. He saw the real Charlie Faye that day. Luckily for you, he was a drunk mess, but your subconscious fear of what he saw has never left you.

The booze, the urine, the cigarettes mixed with the truth. Those smells will always stir up a memory and stay with you forever."

Her words linger in the air like smoke from a blown-out candle. The stale air from Jenny's unopened house, unnoticed to me until now, is putrid. The ambiance of the home has changed in an instant. I want to be here with Jenny. I want to go back to the days of takeout and movies. I long to hear her college stories. My heart aches for Jenny at that moment. I fucked up. I took Jenny away. I miss her. I need her to be here with me. I need her to help me understand, but she isn't here, and the stale reminder of that keeps creeping in as everything in this place turns dustier and older the longer I sit here. I try to focus on the tiny dust particles that shimmer through the soft sparkle the sun is bringing into the living room. I want to shut all of this out. I want to forget again. I'm in my own personal penitentiary.

"Shut up!" I shout as my entire body trembles. "Shut up!"

I begin to pace the room. I'm angry. I'm enraged, and I can't believe what Quinn is saying. "I can't fucking believe you, Quinn. You are such a liar. I don't believe anything that is coming out of your mouth. None of this can be true. Jenny didn't know what she was talking about. You don't know what you are talking about. I hate you all," I scream.

Quinn stares at me. She is just an arm's length away from me, but she doesn't offer me any sort of sympathy or a hug, only continues to watch my break-down.

"None of this is true. That's not how it happened. No, no, no. That's just not right. I don't believe you."

Quinn continues to watch as I process all this information.

Rage is building and moving through my body, starting in my toes, then into my legs, up my torso, and now running through my arms. Before I notice what I'm doing, my weight is now in my right arm and it's pulled behind me, I'm twisted at the hip, and with all my power and rage rushing through that one arm, my palm smacks Quinn against the face with enough force, knocking her to the ground.

"You lie, Quinn. It's all lies. None of this is real," I shout. "You are full of shit! I can't believe you. I'm so tired of your bullshit. I wish you would go away." The room is spinning and I'm dizzy. I feel like the floor is moving below me.

"Get out!" I shout again. "Get the fuck out of here, get the fuck out of my head." My vision is beginning to get darker. A ringing in my ear is getting louder. My eyelids are pulling down against my will.

As my vision is tunneling to a close, I think I see my mom through my darkened haze and hear her crying out for help. Is this real?

"Frank, help, the guest house. Charlie's having another attack." The voice calls out.

My body is lifted and engulfed by a familiar embrace, and soft hands run the length of my head.

"It's OK, my sweet, pretty one, everything is going to be OK. It's all going to be OK now."

"Frank, I think Charlie's little friend is back."

The tunnel is closing in, and all I see is darkness.

# EPILOGUE

### Charlie
### One year later

I've got a lot to sort through after the terrible news I was given today. I don't know if I can handle any more heartbreak. My heart is just not strong enough to endure anymore pain. I'm not sure how long I've been walking, but I find myself down at the park. The park that we used to come to together. I take a seat on an open bench to help clear my mind and try to process what happened.

A pretty girl is walking toward my bench. Please don't sit here. Pick another bench. I want to be alone.

The girl plops down right next to me.

"Oh, I'm sorry. I hope I'm not bothering you. There is nowhere else to sit," the girl says and smiles.

I have a hard time telling her no. I should just get up and leave.

"Beautiful weather we're having, isn't it?"

I nod. It would be rude of me to get up now.

"Is everything OK? You look like you need a friend right now," she says kindly.

I don't want to tell this stranger what's going on, so I just smile back and say, "I'm doing OK." I lie because I'm not ready to talk about it and definitely not to a stranger.

"Well, I'm just going to sit here and if you want to chat. I'm all ears. My name's Quinn by the way."

"I'm Charlie, nice to meet you, Quinn."

# ACKNOWLEDGEMENTS

*The Pretty Ones* wouldn't be a reality if it weren't for all the wonderful people in my life who encouraged, helped, and supported me on this journey.

First, I have to thank my husband, Jeremy. You are my rock, and there is no way this book would have made it to publication without you. From the first day the story was born, you were there through my ups and downs and my constant indecisiveness. You always knew just what to say to keep me going. You believed in me, and for that, I thank you from the bottom of my heart.

To my mom, who has always encouraged me to keep going no matter what hurdle I had to jump over—your words of encouragement on more than one occasion meant the world to me. Thank you for reminding me that it is OK to take a break from time to time.

To my dad, for passing down his love for books and always believing in me.

A huge thank you to my early readers, Rachel, Cody, Taryn, Pam, Stacey, and Sarah. Your excitement and kind words gave me a reason to keep writing. Rachel, I also thank you for your constant ear. Stacey, for your generosity to help a fellow author.

A special thanks to my dear friend Tess, who saw *The Pretty Ones* in its roughest form and still loved it. I couldn't have come this far without your enthusiasm and love for my storytelling. Thank you.

Another special thanks to my friend, Alexis. I will never forget your help getting *The Pretty Ones* over the finish line. Your advice and feedback have been invaluable.

I can't write my acknowledgments without thanking my lovely editor, Rebecca. Thank you for pressing me to see things differently. Your advice and work on my novel really took it to the next level, and for that, I'm beyond grateful.

Another talented soul that I must thank is my cover designer, Natasha, a.k.a Miss Nat Mack. You are brilliant. Thank you for creating the perfect cover that brought *The Pretty Ones* to life.

Finally, I have to say thank you, to you, the reader. You picked up a book from an unknown author and gave me a chance. I am forever grateful. Thank you.

# ABOUT THE AUTHOR

Jamie Lee Fry is an adventure blogger turned psychological thriller writer. When she's not hunched over her desk writing, she's exploring the forests of Oregon with her husband and three dogs. Jamie never says no to a good adventure, as long as mountains and waterfalls are involved. Jamie also enjoys stand-up paddle boarding, kayaking, baking, and documenting life with her camera.

## CONNECT WITH JAMIE:

@Author_JamieLeeFry

www.authorjamieleefry.com

Made in the USA
Monee, IL
27 August 2021

76705759R00173